THE PIT AND THE PENDULUM

BearManor Media
P.O. Box 1129
Duncan, OK 73534-1129

Phone: 580-252-3547
Fax: 814-690-1559

www.bearmanormedia.com

The Pit and the Pendulum adapted by Lee Sheridan
First published as a Lancer Book -1961
The Pit and the Pendulum produced by American International Films
First Bear Manor Edition 2013

Photographs Courtesy of Lawrence French, William Forche and the editor

The Nightmares Series is being published to preserve original movie tie-in novels that were printed in the 1950s and 1960s on the old style pulp paper. Plus a few rare titles where the price of the first editions has put them out of reach for the collectors. We hope these reprints will allow them to last into the new century.

NIGHTMARE SERIES

THE BRIDES OF DRACULA BY DEAN OWEN
THE REVENGE OF FRANKENSTEIN
THE RAVEN - BY EUNICE SUDAK
THE BRIDE OF FRANKENSTEIN BY MICHAEL EGREMONT
DR. CYCLOPS - BY WILL GARTH - SHORT STORY BY HENRY KUTTNER

THE PIT AND THE PENDULUM

Adapted by
Lee Sheridan

From the Richard Matheson Screenplay

The Making of *The Pit and the Pendulum*
By
Lawrence French

Introduction by
Richard A. Ekstedt

Philip J. Riley's

NIGHTMARE SERIES

This volume of the Nightmare series is dedicated to Forry Ackerman, seen above with AIP president, James H. Nicholson & friend.

"THE RAZORS EDGE"
"The Pit and the Pendulum"

By Richard A. Ekstedt

".... The agony of my soul found vent in one loud, long, and final scream of despair."

—EDGAR ALLAN POE

The very first time I ever saw this film, it was not on the big screen at our local movie house, The Lane Theatre, but on the small television tube (in a pan and scan transfer) at my parent's house (Annadale, Staten Island NY) in 1968. To my incredible luck, my folks were out for out for a late evening, and my very Catholic, superstitious, Italian-American mother, who had tried, very unsuccessfully, from having my brain corrupted by watching horror films (she was of the mind-set that such "EVIL" should be violently suppressed, the filmmakers of them brought before a Church Tribunal, be judged guilty, and then burned at the stake!), wasn't going to be able to prevent me from watching the television premier of "The Pit and the Pendulum," starring Vincent Price.

For me, viewing this film, it was Bliss! Rapture!! Ecstasy! What I didn't know at the time, never having had the chance of seeing it on the big screen, was that the opening scene I was watching, before the credits, in the insane asylum, was shot for the television broadcast to pad out the film's running time (this footage, is happy to say, on the DVD as an extra).

Despite, as I mentioned, the image being cramped, being scanned (those ancient dark days before widescreen transfers), I was drawn into this nightmarish story of madness and adultery! My corrupted brain has been fully ever thankful ever since Vincent Price's laugh.

It was some years later, when I started collecting laserdisc (and then, moving on to DVD), that I finally got to view "The Pit and the Pendulum" (and a lot of other Roger Corman movies) as it was meant to be seen in its beautiful widescreen splendor. I was able to really come to appreciate the restoring of the mood, captured so beautifully by Floyd Crosby (who was behind the photography), that was like a sweet nectar for the eyes! The hues: wild and vibrant, matching the dark shades found throughout the film, gave me a deeper appreciation of what director Roger Corman was able to pull off.

When Roger Corman finished filming the highly successful "House of Usher", for American-International, I understand he was not intending to film a series based upon the works of Edgar Allan Poe.

But "Usher" proved to be both, a commercial and critical success, prompting him to do another Poe follow up. Once again, writer Richard ("Incredible

Shrinking Man": novel and film screenplay) Matheson, who did such a grand job on "House of Usher," tackled the job of transforming Poe's tale into an original, intelligent screenplay.

Vincent Price, back for another round of Poe, after playing Roderick Usher in "House of Usher" (getting to play, this time, two roles!), was cast along with an excellent group of actors who were gathered for this new production. John Kerr, in the role of Englishman Frances Barnard, had performed in the classic film, "Tea and Sympathy" (with Deborah Kerr), was recruited to play, in what would be his final film (he went to law school and went on to be a lawyer). Luana Anders, who was a familiar face at American- International (who would also appear in "Dementia 13"), was cast to play Spanish noblewoman, Catherine Medina (the sister of Price's character, Nicholas). Also in the cast was Anthony Carbone, in the role of the family doctor, Charles Leon. But, the biggest name under Vincent Price was the casting of the Dark Queen herself: Barbara Steele! The British actress, fresh from Mario Bava's Italian production of "The Mask of Satan" ("La Maschera del Demonio"), which was issued under the American International banner here, for its U.S. release as "Black Sunday in 1960; projects such an incredible presence, that her aura is felt even in scenes she is not in. The sad drawback in her role was that she was re-dubbed.

The plot to "The Pit and the Pendulum" is simple enough. In 1546, Spain, English aristocrat Frances Barnard (John Kerr) travels to Spain to find out what has happened to his sister (who has died) Elizabeth (Barbara Steele), who is married to a Spanish nobleman, Nicholas Medina (Vincent Price). While Nicholas seems very sincere and is obviously grieving, something does not sit well with Mr. Barnard. There are fears on Nicholas's part of premature burial, which Dr. Leon says is just not possible. Nicholas tells Frances that his wife fell slowly into a deep depression and was given to loss of appetite and lack of sleep. Her nightly wanderings would lead her into the old, abandoned torture chamber, once the horrid workshop of Nicholas's crazed, murderous father, Sebastian Medina (also played by Vincent Price).

Sebastian Medina, a leader in the Spanish inquisition, tortured and murdered Nicholas's adulterous mother, after killing her lover (Sebastian's own brother), in view of young Nicholas, who was hiding and viewed the horrible event. The older Nicholas, still haunted by this memory, is now obsessed that Elizabeth was entombed alive!

The revealed truth at the shattering climax, is the conclusion of a horrible journey for all that will lead into a web of betrayal, madness and murder!

"The Pit and the Pendulum" was a critical and commercial triumph, when released to theatres on August 23, 1961. Running a fluid 85 minutes, Roger Corman and all involved in the production, really enjoyed themselves. The director had commented in "The Films of Roger Corman: Brilliance on a Budget" by Ed Naha (St. Martin's Press, 1996), "I enjoyed "The Pit and the Pendulum" because I actually got the chance to experiment a bit with the movement of camera. There was a lot of moving camera work and interesting cutting at the climax."

As I said much earlier, the very first time I saw this gem was on television. "The Pit and the Pendulum" was broadcast on ABC Television (Channel 7, NY) and I was unaware that it contained a new, filmed for TV introduction. Tamara Asseyev, a production assistant to Roger Corman, filmed a scene where a now totally insane Catherine Medina (Luana Anders, reprising the role), relates the events of what happened (making the story told from the mind of a madwoman). It was quite effective!

The novelization of the film you are now holding in your hand is a brand new printing of the original 1961 Lancer Book publication, that was released at the time of the original theatrical release of "The Pit and the Pendulum". Told in the first person, by Frances Barnard himself, it is a detailed flashback on the events that occurred at the Medina castle. There are very few original paperback editions left in existence, as time and dust have taken their toll on the brittle pages.

Now once again, as with other expeditions into the dust and cobweb-ridden dark abyss of forgotten tomes, our good friend, Philip J. Riley has returned yet again; eyes wide, looking furtively behind him, to bring back to the light of day this tale of Gothic yore.

And I, his ever faithful servant, fighting off the rats (while brushing the dirt, mold and webs outta my hair), wild eyed and drooling; after having seen things mortal eyes should not behold (like a cow, dancing "The Electric Slide", with a little boy wearing a cow-pattern tee shirt, to a song by Barenaked Ladies), is giggling now with insane delight!

So sit back now, you connoisseur of dark diabolical cinema horror... put your feet up... and try to ignore that strange sound of creaking old machinery, now returning to un-life, that is rising from the dark below!

Richard A. Ekstedt
Somewhere on a mountain in PA!

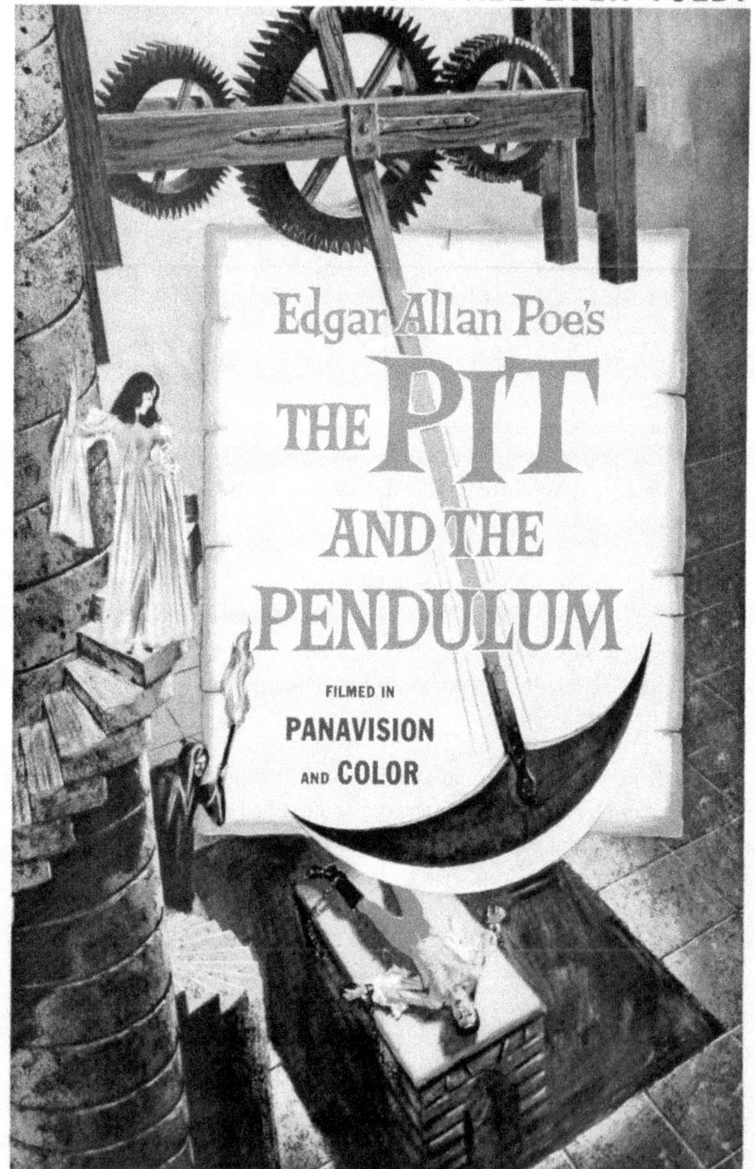
THE GREATEST TERROR TALE EVER TOLD!
Edgar Allan Poe's
THE PIT
AND THE
PENDULUM
FILMED IN
PANAVISION
AND COLOR
STARRING VINCENT PRICE · JOHN KERR · BARBARA STEELE · LUANA ANDERS
SCREENPLAY BY
RICHARD MATHESON
PRODUCED AND DIRECTED BY
ROGER CORMAN
MUSIC BY
LES BAXTER
AN AMERICAN INTERNATIONAL PICTURE

CHAPTER ONE

BY LATE afternoon upon that autumn day in the year 1546, the coach which I had hired that morning was far away from San Sabastian, and I was weary from inactivity as only a healthy young Englishman can become.

After three weeks of travelling, I had passed through a succession of towns and countrysides, in a variety of conveyances, and had encountered every sort of weather. Perhaps it was the errand on which I had come to Spain that made me feel I was leaving sunshine, sweetness—even life, it-self—behind me with every jolting mile of my journey . . . . although I am not usually so fanciful.

In England, my mission to Spain had seemed imperative: the news of my sister's death had reached me indirectly, but after my first comprehension of it, questions had come to my mind. Why? for instance, had such important news come to me roundabout? Was it, perhaps, only rumor? Finally—since, I, Francis Bernard, had become head of the family, following my father's death—I was struck by a most uncomfortable sense of responsibility.

Obviously, it was my duty to either verify or disprove the tale of my sister's death. And so I had set out, not exactly light-heartedly due to the circumstances, but still with a certain irrepressible anticipation. After all, I should be seeing unfamiliar lands, encountering new faces; at the age of 20, I trusted a good many of them might be feminine. . .

In Flanders, there had been sunshine; in France, there were intermittent showers mixed with a golden haze over the vineyards, but as my carriage worked its way tortuously through the mountain passes into Spain, the weather seemed to settle down into a constant and forbidding greyness. Twice I'd been forced to kick my heels for a day in an inferior roadside inn, because the rains made roads impassible—and I had long since discovered that feminine faces are not nearly so attractive under cloudy skies as they are when the sun shines.

I was in a mood now to conclude my business and get back to England as rapidly as possible. With luck, I might be home before the snows and still have time enough for a bit of hawking.

Spurred by this thought, I had ordered four horses put to the hired coach in San Sebastian and told the driver to get the last ounce of speed out of them.

The coachman took me at my word; he used his long curling whip so constantly, thrusting the carriage at near breakneck speed, up and down hills, around curves and splashing through streamlets, that both the horses and I were exhausted. Even in the scattered hamlets we met occasionally, his pace never slackened. I would be roused from an uneasy doze by a strange penetrating bellow from the box. "*Hollaaa* . . .", and glancing from the window, I would see the peasants scattering briskly to safety, right or left, as we swept through. Wryly, I wondered if they thought my coach an imperial messenger of Charles, the Holy Roman Emperor and King of Spain, and I whiled away some of the tedium of the trip by imagining what sort of express news I might be carrying if indeed I were.

We stopped briefly in San Tomas, to ask directions for the road ahead. It was already past four o'clock, and any trace of sunlight had disappeared, although, for the past week at least, I had given up expecting any sunshine in Spain. The atmosphere was heavy and oppressive, threatening a bad storm, and stretching my legs by a turn or two about the coach, I was glad to return to my seat, to close the door and pull my coat collar about my ears.

Shortly, the driver came plodding back to the carriage from the direction of the kitchen yard. Tired and cold as I was, I was immediately conscious of a difference in his temper. Where, before, he had put his back and his strong right arm into whipping on the horses (no doubt inspired by a hint from my previous driver that I was an English idiot but nevertheless generous about tips and an occasional stop for liquid refreshment), now his swarthy face was sullen and closed.

Behind him I could see an array of curious faces, peeping at us from the stableyard, their gaze ranging from frank curiosity to an indescribable expression that seemed almost a superstitious dread. Involuntarily I leaned to the window—and the faces disappeared as swiftly and silently as cats in the snow.

"What's wrong?" I demanded. "Are we on the right road, or have you lost your way like a stupid fellow?"

"No, Señor," he muttered. "The road is correct . . ."

"Then up on your box and be off," I told him, impatiently. "I've had enough of your Spanish roads, I'd like to *arrive* and sit on something solid for a change!"

From the corner of my eye I could see him standing uncertain for a moment, then he plodded to the front of the coach, pulled himself heavily up to his seat, and with a vicious crack of his whip, we were jerked once more into motion.

If anything, the pace was more frantic than before. As I slid from side to side of the seat, every bone in my body ached uncontrollably; even my skin felt sore, and as for the usual bruises one acquires during three weeks of travel—they were sheer agony.

Clinging to the coach strap, I surveyed the sky. It was definitely darker and growing worse by the minute. I thought we were running toward the storm, and that it was going to be a deluge when it broke. Probably, I concluded, that was why the driver was surly.

"He talked with the stableyard peasants," I thought. Peasants are always very knowledgeable about weather; naturally, because their existence depends on it. So now I settled it in my mind that the driver would have preferred to stop for the night in San Tomas, let the storm blow itself out, and drive me the last stage in tomorrow's fair weather. The thought was oddly comforting, for during the day I had found the man rather pleasant.

He had a lusty voice, and as we settled into our journey he sang Spanish songs to the rhythm of the horses' hooves. I had planned to give him a particularly good payment. Certainly he'd earned it in completing the long trip from San Sebastian so quickly. But I found him and his songs very pleasant company, too, and would have been sorry to find, at the end of a tiresome day, the he was only another greedy peasant, after all.

Leaning forward to scan the sky again, I saw at long last my destination. Perhaps it was prophetic that my first view of the Castle Medina should come just as full darkness covered the countryside—and that this countryside (which I had scarcely noticed for the past half hour) should suddenly strike me forcibly as the most barren and desolate I had ever seen.

We were nearing the sea. As the road twisted and turned, I caught glimpses of jagged rocks and foaming surf, beating itself endlessly against the land. Castle Medina stood on a promontory, thrust out into the ocean like an accusing finger. Against the livid sky, it was sinister. Its turrents and battlements reached angrily to the heavens, forever condemned to the earth. I judged it to have been built some three or four hundred years earlier, and unconsciously looked for the moat.

It would, I thought,have been formed from the natural protection of the sea, by the cutting of a rough semicircle around the castle from one side of the ocean front to the other.

Forbidding and inhospitable as it appeared, nevertheless the Castle Medina offered a particular interest to my eyes for this was my sister's home. Tightening my grasp of the coach strap, I gazed, fascinated, as my coach lumbered along.

I quickly identified the moat, and as I surmised, it was a clever use of what Nature had provided. Still, when I thought of the quiet moat about Chipham Manor at home, with its reflective carp and the King's swan that was out proudest possession (Because King Henry himself had given it in recognition of my father's service to the Crown), the moat surrounding Castle Medina was an uncomfortable businesslike affair.

It was apparently deep-set into the land, and when (as now) the ocean was aroused and seething the most water rushed in from both ends simultaneously, meeting violently midway and sending a fountain of spray into the air. Yet, only the tops of the foam could be seen occasionally above the moat banks. I thought the moat must be very deep indeed and mentally congratulated the original designer of Castle Medina.

As I peered through the gloom, with a mixture of revulsion and excitement, the horses suddenly slackened speed and in another few minutes we had stopped. With a start, I pulled myself back to the present.

Beside us was a road leading across a drawbridge and losing itself thereafter in the trees and gloom. No glimmer of light shone from the gatekeeper's cottage facing us, nor was there any human being running forward with a smile of welcome for a visitor. A tongue of lightning split the sky to my left, and suddenly I felt apprehensive.

All the reason for my presence in this unpleasant locality rose compellingly in my mind as I stared at the menacing outlines of the Castle looming over the trees ahead. Simultaneously, the burly figure of my driver appeared and threw open the door.

We are here Señor," he said. "Please to descend."

"What do you mean 'we are here'? This is not the castle, you oaf; it's the gate-keeper's cottage. Put my bags back and take me to the end of the road."

"Please to descend," he repeated stubbornly. This is the Castle Medina; I go no farther."

With a vague idea that perhaps there was, after all, someone from the Castle to convey guests the last few yards, I got out of the coach, groaning slightly as I stretched my tired legs. Instantly, the coachman had slammed the coach door closed behind me and was shambling toward the steps to his driver's box. And looking about, I could see no one waiting to conduct me. *"Here!"* I said to the coachman. "Hola, *there!"* what do you mean by leaving me here? You were hired to drive me to the Castle Medina! This is not the Castle, and there's no one from the estate to take my bags. You'll have to drive me to the Castle entrance."

To my amazement, the man paid no attention. As quickly as possible, he reached the coach and pulled his 200-pounds into the driver's seat.

"Stop!" I said, but he merely picked up his whip and prepared to turn the coach about for the return journey. "You realize you'll get no additional payment for this insolence," I shouted angrily.

As the coach drew abreast of me, headed for San Tomas and San Sebastion, the driver looked down at me strangely. "I want none, Señor," he told me. "What would I do with Devil's gold?"

I stared at him, uncomprehending, while he crossed himself furtively. Then, with a vicious flick of his long whip, he drove away as though fleeing from Hell itself.

I stood alone in the road, watching the retreat of the coach with a mixture of incredulity and objectivity. It seemed to be departing even more rapidly than it had brought me, if such a thing was possible, and while one half of my mind was furiously annoyed by the man's refusal to drive me to the castle door in proper style, I vindictively assessed his chances of getting the empty coach back to San Tomas without overturning it.

As I watched the rickety swaying carriage and the wheels bouncing in and out of the potholes in that apology for a road, I felt his chances were not too good—and took an honest satisfaction in thought of the consequences when he finally returned to San Sebastian with a damaged coach. With a final flick of the whip, the coach vanished around a curve.

I looked about me. I couldn't be sure of the exact time, but I estimated it at about 5 o'clock. I picked up my travelling bags and turned to the drawbridge. My boots rang hollowly in the silence, but there was still no response from the lodge house. I thought it must be deserted and unused, else someone would have come to investigate the altercation between myself and the coachman, so I breathed deeply and plunged ahead into the darkness of the drive.

Five minutes of brisk walking, principally uphill, brought me to the front entrance of the castle, and it was a noble entrance indeed: a flight of shallow marble steps, leading to a majestic entrance patio surrounded by a balustrade and urns of potted trees, neatly clipped.

In the center was the front door, with an immense and intricately carved iron knocker. It was, at first glance, the most inviting thing I had seen, and I strode across the marble courtyard, grasped the knocker and battered it vigorously.

For a moment I stood, expectantly, but there was no sign of life. Setting down my bags, I knocked once more; but for a full three minutes more, there was no response.

True, the family might be away from the castle, but there would certainly be a caretaker—and I would, with equal certainty, expect a full staff of servants. *Someone* should hear a knock at the front door of a castle.

I had raised my hand to knock once more when the door swung open silently, revealing an unmistakable major domo. His hair was grey, but his figure was unexpectedly vigorous.

"Yes?" he said curtly.

"I am here to see Don Medina. My name is . . ." I began, but he merely looked past me into space.

"Don Medina is not receiving visitors at present," he stated, and to my astonishment the door began to swing closed in my face!

"He'll see me," I said coldly. "You will announce that Mr. Francis Barnard is here to call upon him."

For the space of a breath, the door wavered, then it continued to swing toward me. I lost my healthy English temper. Of its own volition, my hand landed flatly against the heave oak, and my foot and leg moved across the threshold.

"Is this the way you always receive relations by marriage?" I asked.

"Be so good as to remove your body, Señor," he said . . . and as I pressed against it and he attempted to close it, I was astonished to realize the strength of the man. I have no idea who might have conquered in our duel, for it was cut short by a feminine voice in the dim-lit hall I had glimpsed behind him.

"Maximilian! What is it?"

With a start, the major domo released the door and stepped back, looking over his shoulder. Approaching us, down a wide staircase, was a girl. Her skin was as fair as that of an English lass, her hair was a chestnut brown with glints of gold under the torches of the wall holders. She wore a fashionably cut gown of deep golden brocade in the Spanish style—that is, with the full skirts built out over the iron petticoats, and the stiffened linen ruff framing her small piquant face. She managed both with the inborn dignity of an *Infanta.*

I'd had no idea who she was, of course, except that she was obviously important. Maximilian simply crumbled and I stepped bodily into the great entrance hall of the Castle Medina.

She came swiftly down the last few steps and faced us. There was complete authority in her voice. "Who is this, Maximilian?" she asked.

"He *demands* to be admitted, Dona," Maximillian's voice took on the age-old whine of any servant caught in a situation too much for him. "I have told him. . . ."

"You are Dona Medina?" I said suddenly, remembering a phrase in an old letter from my sister.

Her eyes surveyed me dispassionately—and I discovered they were the color of the purple-brown pansies in my mother's simple-garden! "I am," she said, with a slight inclination of the head.

"Kindly instruct your servant to admit me . . ."

"He has already received his instructions, sir," she interrupted, "to admit *no one*. Now if you will excuse me . . ."

Turning, she was moving away. Something in her indifference angered me; it was as though she, the daughter of the castle, felt I was an upstart . . . and by Maximilian's covert smile as the door began to swing shut, I sensed he was savoring the situation. I could change that, I knew—and I did.

"One moment, Dona Medina," I said. "I am Francis Barnard . . ." She hesitated briefly, her back still turned to me, then she made a small gesture of her hand and I sensed she would move on her way, so I turned the knife that I had struck to her heart by merely my name. I am Elizabeth's brother," I said. "*You remember Elizabeth?*"

CHAPTER TWO

FOR AN instant, the great hall seemed timeless, suspended in some great void of nothing. I had not wanted to hurt the girl. I had not wanted her stricken, trembling, fighting for composure . . .yet she was all these things—and then, superbly under control within a minute.

When she turned to me, her face was calm. She came toward me once more, while Maximillian drew himself into the semblance of a formal mojor domo. I still thought she managed the iron petticoat frame with incredible grace—and that she might have been even lovelier without it.

"Elizabeth's brother," she said softly. "Ah, forgive me, if you can. How was I to know?" Her eyes fixed on mine, she made a small gesture toward my battered travelling bags. "Maximilian!" Like an automaton, the major domo moved to the bags, as she came to stand before me.

"Please forgive me," she said again. "I am Catherine Medina."

"Dona," I replied formally, and bent to kiss her hand. It was as cold as the grave. I released it quickly and stepped back, as Maximilian picked up the bags and started away. "No, leave them here!"

Silently he set them down again, and closed the big front door behind me, as Catherine Medina protested, "But of course you will spend the night with us, Mr. Barnard! I am certain my brother will wish it."

"Perhaps," I told her, and by the widening of her eyes, I saw that my coolness had reached her.

She seemed anxious to make up, by sudden cordiality, for the former lack of welcome, but I was not so sure I wanted any hospitality from the Medinas. Her words might grow warmer, but her hand had been cold as the chill I felt in the castle itself. Still, I had to conclude the business that had brought me to Spain. Handing my cloak and hat to Maximilian, I went on, "May I see your brother now?"

"He is—resting, Mr. Barnard. He has not been well since . . ." A graceful gesture indicated that she would rather not talk of a family tragedy.

So it was *true* that my sister was dead! Coldly, I persisted. "Ah? And when may I see him?"

"Perhaps at supper, if you would do us that honor?"

"Very well. At supper, then." My tone left no doubt that I was prepared to wait until supper and not a minute longer. Her eyes slid away from mine and studied the cold marble floor briefly, while Maximilian silently bore away my cloak and vanished through a door in the paneling.

Turning away from her deliberately, I struggled to maintain control of myself. The confirmation of Elizabeth's death still left questions unanswered, and I was furiously angry, both at the insolence of the Medinas in failing to send any formal word to Elizabeth's family and at the coldness I had received and was still receiving.

Granted that Don Medina, as a sorrowing widower, might refuse to see visitors in general, *I* was no casual caller. Although I had seen little of Elizabeth, who was older than I and who had been sent, after our mother's death when I was 13, to live with relatives in France, I was nevertheless her brother. On that score alone, I should have been welcomed with warmth and an interruption of my brother-in-law's "rest."

Looking about the great entrance hall, half of my mind considered these conflicting emotions while the other half observed the display of old-fashioned armor, the tilting lances, and iron braziers which might, if they had contained any fire, have removed some of that deadly chill. If this was Spanish grandeur, I wanted no part of it.

Catherine Medina was still standing motionless before me, her eyes fixed on the floor, and with an impulse to wound her, I said formally, "If I might see my sister's graven then, before supper?"

"Grave?" she said, startled.

"I presume there is one?"

"Not as such," she replied. Elizabeth;in interred . . ." again the light graceful gesture of a hand, ". . . below."

"Interred?"

She drew her small figure erect; I had to admire her regal command of herself. "That is the family custom of the Medinas, Mr. Barnard," she told me superbly.

"I see," I said politely. "Then—if we may go there?"

Her hesitation was so brief that only my newborn suspicion could have been aware of it; but with a formal smile, she said, "Of course. Please follow me."

We walked across the great hall and down a narrow stairway I had not noticed before. It led us into a lower corridor, lined with wall brackets, each containing a torch whose flames flickered wildly in the icy draft. It was an eerie place of long shadows, and the chill raised a new question.

Catharine's small figure moved ahead of me. To her back I said, "When did Elizabeth die? My information made no mention of the exact date."

"It was about three months ago."

"Three months!" I felt stunned. "And may I ask," I said tightly, "why I was notified sooner?"

Her shoulders quivered slightly. "I—" she murmured, but I interrupted angrily, "How did Elizabeth die?"

She paused momentarily, and I came abreast of her. "I know very little of the details, I'm afraid. This is no longer my home, you see. I left it several months before Nicholas married your sister."

"You don't even know how . . ." I began incredulously, and stopped. It would have been impossible to continue, in any case, for my words could not have been heard in the sudden clamor that struck my ears.

Shrill, oscillating with an ear-splitting whine, the noise increased and reverberated from the walls of the narrow corridor in which we stood. About us, the wall torches vibrated and beneath my feet the stones of the floor trembled.

"What in the name of Heaven . . ." I began, but Catherine Medina stood her ground, though her face was waxen white.

"This way, Mr. Barnard," she said, and made to move forward, but I caught her arm.

"What is that noise?" I demanded.

Her lips trembled as she stared at me, but it was evident that she could think of nothing to say. Slipping from my grasp, she could think of nothing to say. Slipping from my grasp, she continued along the corridor. I looked at her rigidly-held shoulders in astonishment. Did she intent to *ignore* this hideous sound? It seemed that she did! I strode after her; I had no wish to be abandoned in the basement of Castle Medina, alone with that terrifying noise, and from the determination of Catherine's steps, I realized she was entirely willing to walk away and leave me to find my own path.

She had moved a considerable distance, I found, and had passed the entrance to a side corridor. In my anxiety to catch up with her, I had nearly missed the opening . . . but it seemed that the noise had its source there.

"Dona Medina!" I shouted imperatively, and, still turned from me, she halted reluctantly, while I surveyed the corridor. It was not very long, furnished with the usual array of flickering wall torches. Facing me, at the end of the stone floor, was an immense heavy door. Unquestionably, the noise that still surrounded and deafened us lay behind that door.

Impulsively, I started toward it. Behind me, Catherines's voice said, "Not that way, Mr. Barnard! but I ignored her.

I felt, rather than heard, that she had turned and was following me swiftly. Nor was there any doubt that something malignant lay ahead of me, for the noise grew louder and louder until it maddened me with a superstitious dread. Then, suddenly, as I had nearly reached the door, the vibrating whine slowed and stopped.

Automatically, I halted, and Catherine came up beside me. "Mr. Barnard, please!"

The arrogance of her voice annoyed me. After all, my sister had lived here; here, she had died—but what sort of home could she have had, filled with unfeeling people and all the noises if Hell? I meant to find out, and brushing Catherine's detaining hand from my arm, I forced myself to walk forward deliberately.

For a moment I hesitated, listening. Now, there was only silence, and I will not deny that I had very nearly turned away to follow Catherine Medina once more—for what dread spectacle might lie behind that door?—when I shook off my impulse to cowardice. Bracing myself, I stretched my hand to the carved metal door handle and felt it move.

Violently, it tore itself from my trembling fingers and swung wide, to reveal a man. So closely we faced each other that instinctively we recoiled.

Very tall and extremely handsome, with an impeccably trimmed mustache in the Spanish manner, his dark eyes burned into mine as he caught himself by one strong hand against the door frame.

For a long moment we stared at each other. Then he drew himself up with menacing formality and demanded, "*Who are you?*"

CHAPTER THREE

BEFORE I could reply, Catherine Medina stood beside me. "This is Mr. Barnard, Nicholas." Did I imagine a warning note in her soft voice as she added, "Elizabeth's *brother,* Nicholas.

There was no doubt he was startled. "Ah?" With the same regal ease I'd already encountered in Catherine Medina, he controlled himself and extended his hand. "You are welcome, sir."

But my slow English temper was beginning to boil, and I ignored his hand. Turning to Catherine, I inquired with the most delicate sarcasm at my command," 'Resting,' Dona Medina?"

"Sir?" Nicholas Medina was completely at sea, but from Catherine's quick-drawn breath and faintly blushed face, I knew I had hit home.

"I told Mr. Barnard you were resting, Nicholas," she murmured. "I—thought you were."

Smiling blandly, Nicholas Medina stepped forward into the corridor, pulling the door shut behind him. Producing an immense key, he bent his great height slightly to fit it in the door, and as if it were the most ordinary thing in the world, locked the room. The click of the lock reminded me . . .

"That noise, sir . . . ?"

"Oh, merely—an apparatus, Mr. Bernard." My brother-in-law casually tucked the key in a pocket of his handsomely embroidered black velvet doublet, and just as casually abandoned the point. "And what brings you to us? he inquired politely.

I stared at him, thunderstruck. "What *brings* me . . ." I began, but he continued smoothly, ". . . though you would ever be welcome, sir."

With a fleeting memory of my arrival at Castle Medina, I lost the remains of my temper. "Elizabeth was my *sister,* Don Medina! I received a report . . . roundabout and unverified . . . of her untimely death. It was a report entirely devoid of details . . . perhaps, only a rumor. . . . What should I have done, as head of the Bernard family—remained comfortably at home in England?"

Nicholas Medina shifted uncomfortably, his face suddenly tormented. "You are quite right, sir," he admitted. "I owe you my apologies. Shock and grief restrained me from more adequate communication." His dark eyes closed unhappily. "You have every right to be provoked."

Before his obvious pain and desolation, I felt unable to sustain my anger. "Then, if I may see my sister's . . . place of internment now?"

The dark eyes flew open in bewilderment, turned on Catherine.

"I thought it would all right, Nicholas," she said.

He was himself again in a moment. "Of course, my dear," he reassured her with a gentle smile. "Mr. Barnard has every right . . . If you will return to the main corridor, sir, I will conduct you."

In silence, we moved away from the heavy door concealing the "apparatus," but in the turmoil of my mind I had already nearly forgotten the Hellish noise. Intent upon my own thoughts, I said, as we turned once more along the stone floor I had traversed with Catherine Medina, "Perhaps, sir, *you* will be good enough to tell me how my sister died?"

I did not miss the almost imperceptible exchange of glances between Nicholas and his sister, nor her faint nod of the head, but it conveyed nothing to me.

"It was an illness of some duration, sir."

"And was this illness diagnosed?" I asked.

"Yes, of course," Nicholas Medina replied.

"By whom?"

"Dr. Leon, a physician of repute."

"And he decided . . . ?"

My brother-in-law (though with every moment of his acquaintance I was liking the relationship less) shrugged evasively. "Something in her blood."

"In her *blood?*" My own blood rushed to my head. Was the man implying something was wrong with the Barnard heritage? "And that was the complete diagnosis—just 'something' in her blood?"

"I am afraid so," he returned calmly, continuing along the corridor. I glanced quickly at Catherine, walking beside me, but her face was half-turned from me and her eyes were fixed studiously on the stone floor.

"And I am afraid that does not satisfy me, sir," I said.

He turned slowly, and I saw before us another narrow stairway leading downward. Again I caught that nearly-imperceptible flicker of a glance between brother and sister, but he said only, "This way, Mr. Barnard."

Silently, I passed him and started down the steps. My boots rang harshly on the stone, and chill air seemed to rush up to envelop me in a foretaste of some horror to come. At the bottom of the steps, I faced a heavy iron door; two wall torches flickered in the wrought-iron brackets on either side, and high on the left-hand doorpost hung a huge key.

My eyes fastened upon this in fascination, for keys have always seemed a symbol and a superstition to me. What may they not unlock and release to our frightened gaze—or happy anticipation.

Politely, Nicholas reached past me to take down the key, which he inserted in the door and turned. With some effort, he pushed back the iron barrier and I was struck once more by the strength of the man. For all the apparent languor of him, he was no weakling.

With a groan, the door to the crypt swung back and the dank air rushed into my nostrils—fetid as the breath of a boar taken in the hunt. I felt nauseated by the smell of death, but Nicholas Medina reached up unconcernedly to grasp one of the blazing wall flambeaux and with a courteous gesture, ushered me onward.

Despite my horror, I looked curiously about the crypt. It was a large open chamber, walled in stone with metal plaques of varying sizes embedded more or less evenly in the walls. There were no caskets, and at last I realized the meaning of Catherine Medina's expression "internment" . . .

Behind each plaque, bricked into the walls, were the tombs of the Medinas, hidden from sunlight and the eyes of men.

Controlling my distaste, I followed my brother-in-law and his sister. They moved slowly through the chamber, and halted. Nicholas gestured slightly, and held the torch high, and my unwilling eyes encompassed freshly placed bricks, a wall plaque bright with newness.

It was incised in sharp letters: ELIZABETH MEDINA, 1517-1546.

I drew in my breath sharply and glanced at my companions. Catherine's eyes met mine and with an anxious, almost pleading gaze; Nicholas, on the other hand, held the torch in a steady hand, but his eyes were veiled from me in the darkness: he was obviously unable to bring himself to look at the tomb.

"Elizabeth is behind this wall?" I asked after a moment. Nicholas nodded, his eyes still averted.

"Why?" I demanded.

"The custom of our family," he muttered.

Catherine leaned forward to touch my sleeve urgently. "May we go now, Mr. Barnard? This is very painful for my brother."

"And for me, as well, Dona Catherine," I reminded her bluntly. Her hand dropped from my arm.

"I assure you, sir, it is no more than the Medina tradition," Nicholas told me, his voice trembling faintly. "Will you stay the night with us?"

"The night—and more," I told him meaningfully, "until I know exactly what has happened here, sir."

Without waiting for his reply, I turned to the door of the crypt and walked firmly into the outer corridor. The air seemed fresher here, and I ascended the steps with a deliberate tread. Catherine Medina caught up to me in the upper corridor. "Please, Mr. Barnard, she said breathlessly, "try to understand.

"I am not deficient in intellect, Dona Catherine," I told her stiffly, "but when understanding is asked, it is as well to have all the facts revealed at the same time—and you will admit that in the present instance I have reason to complain that I have not been given facts."

She glanced at me briefly. "Are you so sure, Mr. Barnard, that facts are the *only* requirement for understanding?"

"Upon what else can anything be based?"

"Oh—many things," she shrugged. But I was in no mood to cope with her provocative words. Actually, I felt certain they were no more than the usual feminine conversation that seems always designed to distract the masculine mind from essentials, and correspondingly, I resented the obvious effort to soothe me and allay my suspicions.

At that moment, I did not have any specific thoughts, but with every passing moment in Castle Medina I had become more certain that *something* existed which should be suspected—should be revealed and destroyed!

We had been walking along the stone corridor; now we reached a door, and with a thrust of my arm I opened it, to step again into the great entrance hall.

Inwardly, I was pleased that my English flair for direction sustained me, even in the underground labyrinth beneath a Spanish castle.

My travelling bags still sat forlornly on the stone slabs; Catherine's light footsteps pattered beside me, and simultaneously, as if summoned by the Devil, Maximilian emerged from a door in the opposite wall.

He moved purposefully toward the entrance door, and I took a mean satisfaction in his reaction when Catherine Medina said, "Take Mr. Bernard's bags, Maximilian, and conduct him to his chamber.

Startled, he turned slowly and looked me up and down, his swarthy face dour and resentful. Then he bent to pick up my bags, and silently moved to the main staircase, while Dona Catherine continued her instructions.

"The Portrait Room, Maximilian. . . . And you will conduct Mr. Barnard to the dining room at supper-time."

Turning toward me, she said formally, "I will take leave of you for the moment, Mr. Barnard. I trust you will rest before joining us again, and if there is anything you wish, Maximilian will be at your service. . . . you understand, Maximilian?"

The servant jerked his head briefly, without looking at her, and continued up the stairs. Not to be outdone by her formality, I bowed and sketched the kiss on the hand, dropping it with indifference. "Your servant, Dona . . ." Then I rapidly followed Maximilian, who was already half-way up the long staircase and evidently not going to wait for my courtesies.

We emerged into an upper hall, stretching across the castle (as near as I could judge), and here at least there was some attempt at comfort. The wall flambeaux were set low enough for a lady's hand to grasp; the floor was covered by soft carpets in glowing designs, and the door through which Maximilian presently ushered me was richly carved of deeply-polished wood.

The room within was large and luxuriously furnished, yet with a repellent coldness in the formality of its appointments. A healthy fire leaped and hissed in the huge carved marble fireplace, but contributed nothing to the chill in the air. Wordlessly, Maximilian deposited my battered bags and had vanished through the door while I was yet assessing my chamber. I could only hope that he would return, as directed, to conduct me to the supper room when the proper time arrived.

Inwardly, I was pleased that my English flair for direction sustained me, even in the underground labyrinth beneath a Spanish castle.

My travelling bags still sat forlornly on the stone slabs; Catherine's light footsteps pattered beside me, and simultaneously, as if summoned by the Devil, Maximilian emerged from a door in the opposite wall.

He moved purposefully toward the entrance door, and I took a mean satisfaction in his reaction when Catherine Medina said, "Take Mr. Bernard's bags, Maximilian, and conduct him to his chamber.

Startled, he turned slowly and looked me up and down, his swarthy face dour and resentful. Then he bent to pick up my bags, and silently moved to the main staircase, while Dona Catherine continued her instructions.

"The Portrait Room, Maximilian. . . . And you will conduct Mr. Barnard to the dining room at supper-time."

Turning toward me, she said formally, "I will take leave of you for the moment, Mr. Barnard. I trust you will rest before joining us again, and if there is anything you wish, Maximilian will be at your service. . . . you understand, Maximilian?"

The servant jerked his head briefly, without looking at her, and continued up the stairs. Not to be outdone by her formality, I bowed and sketched the kiss on the hand, dropping it with indifference. "Your servant, Dona . . ." Then I rapidly followed Maximilian, who was already half-way up the long staircase and evidently not going to wait for my courtesies.

We emerged into an upper hall, stretching across the castle (as near as I could judge), and here at least there was some attempt at comfort. The wall flambeaux were set low enough for a lady's hand to grasp; the floor was covered by soft carpets in glowing designs, and the door through which Maximilian presently ushered me was richly carved of deeply-polished wood.

The room within was large and luxuriously furnished, yet with a repellent coldness in the formality of its appointments. A healthy fire leaped and hissed in the huge carved marble fireplace, but contributed nothing to the chill in the air. Wordlessly, Maximilian deposited my battered bags and had vanished through the door while I was yet assessing my chamber. I could only hope that he would return, as directed, to conduct me to the supper room when the proper time arrived.

Meanwhile, I felt glad of some time in which to take stock of the situation.

The confusions and suspicions in my mind must be considered and, if possible, set at rest—yet this sensible decision was immediately destroyed by the discovery (which I made at once) that my door possessed neither key nor bolt. I spent some minutes thereafter in hunting out from my baggage the beautiful daggers of finely tempered steel which I'd been unable to resist on my journey through Toledo. There was also, I noted, a sturdy chair of painted wood, suitable for placing under the curving brass door handle. I could only trust that I might not be so overtired that night as to sleep through any possible attempt to enter my room.

At length I poured myself a glass of wine from the fine crystal decanter on the side table. One sip confirmed that Don Medina had a nice taste in wines, but only increased my confusion: a room obviously prepared for a guest, fire alight and the choicest wine set forth—yet this scarcely agreed with the evident surprise and surliness of Maximilian, when he was ordered to convey me here.

Most of all, I wondered at the absence of bolt or key. . . . and threw myself back against the cushions, flexing my weary legs. For several minutes, I sipped the wine and gave myself up to a half-hypnotized contemplation of the flickering flames. In another minute, I might have been asleep—but the unanswered questions plagued me and brought me alive again.

I had come into Spain, at considerable expense of time and trouble, on a journey that *should* have been unnecessary. What, at this moment, had I discovered.

That my sister had died more than three months previously, that she was walled in behind bricks and mortar in a subterranean crypt, which was "a family custom of the Medinas". No one, it seemed could tell me why Elizabeth should have died in the first place—nor could anyone explain, to my satisfaction, why a formal letter giving all the details should not have been dispatched in so long a period by *someone.* Even if Nicholas were truly demented by grief, surely Catherine . . . or this doctor. . . .

What ever I learned seemed only to lead to other questions, and it was no part of my quest to disrupt and shatter the Medinas needlessly. Yet I meant to know the truth before I left this gloomy spot, no matter what the cost in human emotions.

Refilling my wine glass, I considered facts and events.

What did I *know* of Nicholas Medina? No more than that my aunt had written some years previous to inform us of my sister's approaching marriage to a wealthy Spaniard of the highest degree. . . but I could not help recalling that I had always thought (after one meeting with my aunt) that she was a trifling woman who had absorbed all the worst of her ducal French husband's frippery notions.

Her letter had been more concerned with emphasizing *her* indispensable office in contracting the marriage that with Elizabeth and her possible happiness. Had Elizabeth, in fact, *been* happy? Could anyone be happy in the Castle Medina? Cold, inhospitable, damp and formal—perhaps Elizabeth had drooped and died like an English daisy.

I felt torn between a desire to leave Castle Medina at once, and my responsibility as head of the Barnard family. One the one hand, I had known

Elizabeth only slightly. It was possible that the strange coldness I had encountered was merely Spanish formality among aristocrats. But on the other hand, I knew I could not rest without knowing every detail of her death.

Deeply troubled, I rose from my seat and paced before the fire. It was when I straightened from tossing a fresh log into the flames that I became aware of the two paintings above the high, intricately carved marble mantel. Then I knew why Dona Catherine had spoken of the "Portrait Room."

Framed in identical heavy golden strips, there was a haunting similarity between the faces. To the left was a man who might have been Nicholas Medina, but that his face was more gaunt and menacing. His ashen skin was doubly emphasized by the black robe and skull cap he wore.

The right-hand painting was evidently of the same family, with clothes of rich red hues, setting off the dark skin and eyes. Again I was conscious of unease, of malign influences at work, although the costumes were of a cut 50 years out of fashion, and unquestionable both of the men in the portraits were long dead. . .

"Perhaps they are interred below?" I thought, and if I had summoned them from the underworld, a hollow knock resounded, resounded upon my chamber door.

"Yes?" I called, and with a sense of foreboding, watched the great door swing silently, slowly, open.

CHAPTER FOUR

IT WAS Nicholas Medina. He had donned a surcoat of black velvet lined in white (which I remembered the Spanish considered equal to black for mourning clothes), and richly embroidered with pearls and diamonds. Famed in the door way, I thought I could understand why any woman might accept him for a husband and think herself lucky to get a man of such prepossing aspect, such obvious wealth and taste. All too many young women were glas to take far less, and Elizabeth's dowry had not been grand.

"I—trust you will be comfortable in here," he said, uncertainly, and I was so struck by his indecisive manner—whether to go or stay, standing halfway into a room in the castle of which he was master—that, I could find no reply.

My eye caught the paintings. "Is this you?" I asked, gesturing to the left hand portrait. My question only disconcerted him further.

"What?" he said, advancing a few paces. "Oh no, no—my father. That is Sebastian Medina; the other portrait is that of my uncle."

"Sebastian Medina," I repeated stupidly. "That name is familiar . . ." but he gave me no chance to search for the reference I might have dredged from my memory.

"Mr. Barnard," he said with the courageous determination of a fearful man, "I am—painfully aware of your distrust regarding Elizabeth's death. Please believe me: there is nothing to suspect—*nothing*. I adored your sister. Her death was and is anguish to me." His fine-boned had groped for support, found the back of a chair, clutched it till the knuckles whitened, as he continued, "I beg of you—I beg of you, Mr. Barnard—do not add to my misery."

"I have no wish to distress anyone, Don Medina," I told him, "but you must realize that your word is not enough. . . Not under the circumstances. No," I went on, watching his eyes riveted to mine with the beginning of anger, I am neither insolent nor attacking your honor as a Spanish gentleman, sir. But you must admit that many things need full explanation before I as Elizabeth's brother and had of the house of Barnard can be satisfied that what you say is complete and true."

For a moment he hesitated, his eyes downcast and his hand trembling against the chair, and I suspected that perhaps his real difficulty in life was always the weakness of indecision. I wondered how Elizabeth could have put up with him. She was ever one to admire courage and sense of adventure.

"Please come with me," said Nicholas at last, turning to the door. The sudden authority of his tone gave me pause, but inevitably I followed him as he led the way without a backward glance, down the corridor to another carved door. Throwing it open, he indicated I was to enter. Still with authority, he walked across the dim interior to throw aside the heavy curtains at the windows.

With my first cursory glance I understood. This had been Elizabeth's room, sumptuously furnished. A door in the farther wall evidently led to the sleeping chamber. Nicholas moved about as though here he was at home and master of himself.

"The air grows heavy," he said casually, and strode over to open a window. Turning back to me, he remarked, "This was her room, Mr. Barnard. I have kept it exactly as she left it"

"Why have you brought me here?"

"Look more carefully about you, sir."

At his command, I looked more critically at the furnishings. Since he seemed to expect, even to demand my compliance, I moved closer to examine the trinkets and neat appointments of the chamber. Behind me, Nicholas continued in a resonant voice I had not know he possessed.

"This room was furnished and arranged with dedicated love. Every article of furniture you see, every tiny trinket, every decorative feature, is the work of the finest artisans in Spain, Italy, France—indeed, from every country of the civilized world."

Wandering slowly from chair to table, from fireplace to flambeau holder, I could well believe his words. Chipham Manor in England possessed its own treasures, but none to compare with these. Velvety floor coverings such as I had never seen bloomed and glowed in a riot of color beneath my feet; I thought perhaps they were brought from the East, for I had heard of the cunning weavers among the Saracens.

A harpsichord of fine-polished wood was well-placed to catch the light from the long windows. It was covered with an exquisitely embroidered shawl of Chinese design. Music sheets still stood against the stand, and the keys were of the purest ivory.

Carved chests and wardrobes must have contained more fine linen and silken gowns than were owned even by one of Harry Tudor's queens. Dazedly, and quite unconscious of my rudeness, I lifted the lid of a square, silver table box—to be stunned by a blaze of diamonds, precious rubies and sapphires.

Truly, it seemed my sister had possessed everything to delight a woman's heart, and for all the strange combination of weakness and physical strength that I had sensed in Nicholas Medina, I thought him a man most capable of pleasing a woman. Of course, he was not English. . . .

"This is a room beyond compare," Nicholas told me. "It is unique—irreplaceable. . . ."

Looking about me, I could only agree. Yet a coldly practical thought came to my mind. True, the room was exquisite, perfect in every detail, but from the note of satisfaction in Don Medina's deep voice, I suspected his aesthetic taste would demand equal perfection in any chamber of the Castle.

"So?" I remarked.

"I did all this for *her,*" my brother-in-law replied, "because I loved her so. . . . because I wanted her to have what no one else in this entire world could have." His eyes lingered on a small inlaid table, set with mother of pearl in an intricate design. With a sweeping gesture of his hand, he said in a pleading voice, "Does not this indicate to you, at least in some small measure, my absolute devotion to your sister?"

Why is he unable to call her Elizabeth? I wondered, and thc thought lent asperity to my answer. "You are a wealthy man, Don Medina. To me, the expenditure of your wealth is no proof of what you call absolute devotion."

His face crumpled with distress as he sought for wards, but before he could do more than mumble disjointedly, "But sir . . . you must realize . . ." we were interrupted by the click of metal. In the silence of the room, it resounded like a canon ball.

I had been facing Nicholas Medina, but the look of sudden horror in his face whirled me about.

I will not deny my own sense of foreboding as I saw that the door to Elizabeth's sleeping chamber was opening slowly! But the effect on Nicholas Medina was catastrophic and out of all proportion to the event. He stood, gape-mouthed as an idiot, frozen with some inner emotion; one hand gripped the lapel of his surcoat with such force that every vein and cord stood out in a bulge of sheer terror.

Despite my own determination for calm and common sense, my spine tingled as I turned again to the opening door. What did Nicholas dread? What should I see in that entrance-way?

With a sudden jerk, the heavily carved door swung wide to reveal—only the back of a servant, accompanied by dusting cloths and a basin of cleaning water!

CHAPTER FIVE

GARBED in the usual coarse linen dress of a servant, with a starched cap covering her black hair, she was obviously quite unaware of our presence. Humming softly, she dusted the carved door panels, picked up the water pail and cleaning cloths, and stepped backward, admiring her own handiwork before extending a sturdy peasant arm to close the door.

Then she turned and saw us—and uttered a scream of terror.

"Maria!" he said, touching his face with trembling fingers and weak with relief. But I wondered whom he had *expected* to see?

"Oh, sir—I beg pardon, sir," her rough voice stumbled in its Spanish dialect. "Oh, sir, you startled me—I was cleaning. . . ."

"Of course," Nicholas told her faintly, and gestured to the outer door. The girl gripped her cleaning aids in firm fingers and with a quick curtsey made for the hall. But I did not miss her frightened glance at her master nor the slight sigh of relief as she let herself quietly out of the room.

Nicholas Medina seemed quite unaware of his effect on Maria. Somewhat recovered, he had moved to the huge fireplace and was drawing back the covering from the over-mantel. I had thought those silken draperies must conceal a painting and I hadn't been mistaken; now I saw that it was one of my sister Elizabeth.

As if drawn by a magnet, I moved forward to seek the best vantage

point for viewing the picture. It had been seven full years since I had seen Elizabeth, but though she had even then been a full-formed and lovely woman in the seven years' time she had become the essence of beauty.

Instinctively I sighed, "Ahhh!"

"God be my witness, Mr. Barnard—I *worshipped* her," Nicholas Medina said behind me. And added brokenly, so soft I could scarce hear the words, "I worship her still."

For the first time I felt inclined to believe him. Impossible for a man not to worship that woman in the portrait with her heart-shaped face, pointed chin, and sleek black wealth of hair. Her brilliant dark eyes looked from under winged black brows, tilted upward at the corners with fascination and mystery.

Her slim pointed fingers lay easily upon her lap, but with an effect of fine-tempered steel that I knew would be equally in command of a mettlesome riding mare as a lute. They were, in fact, like our mother's hands, with the pronounced crooked joint in the middle finger of the left hand. And like our mother—rather than seeking to hide the slight deformity, Elizabeth had drawn attention to it by wearing a superb ring.

It was of two great burning jewels: an emerald, mated with a diamond, each surrounded by pearls, set in finest gold. A memorable ring, fit to lie with the crown jewels of the Alhambra.

So this was Elizabeth grown up. Standing transfixed before the painting, I felt a pride in this daughter of the Barnards, and a desolation in the knowledge that she was gone forever. Behind me, Nicholas paced restlessly about the room.

"Life is meaningless without her, Mr. Barnard," he said distractedly. "Everything is fruitless, utterly devoid of purpose." Briefly, he paused beside me to gaze at the portrait, then moved away so aimlessly that he stumbled into one of the charming inlaid tables. "The beauty," he said, as if to himself alone. "Dear God—the infinite, incredible beauty of her.

There was no mistaking the pain in his voice; it was real, and true, and slowly my suspicions began to melt. "She was the very substance of loveliness," said Nicholas, and I began reluctantly to believe in him as a despairing widower.

Yes, truly my sister, had been incredibly beautiful, and I could understand, dimly, the effect of that beauty on a man such as Nicholas Medina—whose tasteful eye appreciated form, shape, color, grace. He cam up beside me now, laid an arm lightly across my shoulders as any brother-in-law might do, and together we looked at Elizabeth. In the dimness of the oil-light, the painting seemed to vibrate with life and passion; the sparkling diamonds swinging from the tiny ears were not more vital than the glowing ruby velvet of her gown.

"The way she walked and moved," Nicholas said. "Her smile, her voice—she sang like an angel—and played the harpsichord as no woman I have ever known has played it."

His fingers bore painfully into my arm and I sensed he'd forgotten my presence entirely, was talking only to himself. "Each night after we had dined, she would play for me . . . that was my dessert."

Suddenly he swung away from me, buried his face in his hands. "Forgive me, sir. I—had not intended so—to display my emotions. I wanted only to convince you. . . ." His hand gestured to the door. "If you would leave me, for a while. . . ."

Automatically I turned to the door, half-assured there was not, after all, any basis for suspicion, and half reluctant to leave Don Medina alone in such a torment of grief. Uneasily, I recalled tales of men who had taken their own lives in an excess of loneliness.

He seemed completely to have forgotten me. Turning to the fireplace,he crossed his arms on the mantel and with a final glance at Elizabeth's portrait, had hid his face with a groan against his arms.

There seemed nothing to do but to leave him. As quietly as possible, I moved to the door; there I hesitated a while, for I would never wish on Judgement Day, that Our Lord should say of me "You failed to help your human brother."

I glanced again at Elizabeth's portrait above the fireplace and tried to ignore the bowed figure below—when of a sudden the storm that had threatened so many hours broke in all its fury. The fine velvet window draperies billowed inward in the rush of elemental fury, and catching a small table in their passage, smashed a vase into fragments against the floor.

With an unearthly cry, Nicholas Medina whirled around his face contorted with fright. Then, identifying the cause of the noise, he made his way to the window and closed it, replacing the draperies with feverish haste. Then he moved back toward the fireplace, stumbling and catching himself occasionally against one or another of the fine pieces of furniture. He seemed unaware of my continued presence, and though I felt that my intrusion was unwarranted, I could not persuade myself to leave until I was assured he was himself again.

With the closing of the window and drawing of the draperies, Nicholas seemed more calm. His step, in returning to the fireplace, was firmer and more decisive, and his back held more erectly. I thought it safe to depart and quietly opened the door. I had slipped partway through, before turning for a final glance at my brother-in-law.

Once more he stood before the fireplace portrait of Elizabeth. "Be at peace," he urged softly. Then his voice intensified and resounded in the room as he literally begged, *"For God's Sweet Sake, be at peace, Elizabeth!"*

CHAPTER SIX

"YOU LIVE in London, Mr. Barnard?" asked Catherine Medina, trying to make conversation over the supper table.

"Yes," I said. "And you?"

"In Barcelona, with an aunt."

"And—have you been here long?"

"A little more than a week," she said quietly. "I came to be with Nicholas, because . . ."

Her soft voice was lost in the insistent clamor of the front door knocker resounding through the castle. The sudden noise penetrated the melancholy silence of my host, Nicholas Medina. Dazedly he looked up from the food with which he had been toying.

"Who can that be?" Catherine asked involuntarily, then caught herself quickly. "Dr. Leon?"

Again, I intercepted the tiny exchange of glances between brother and sister. Nicholas stood up quickly, pushing back his high carved master-chair with a vigorous thrust. Turning to the door, he reached it in two strides and had thrown it wide, revealing the great entrance hall, into which Maximilian was admitting a visitor.

"Ah, good evening, Maximilian."

"Good evening, Dr. Leon," Maximilian bowed low, quickly too the proffered cloak and hat—what a different reception from my own, some hours previously!

He was a handsome man of middle height and middle age, rather more fashionably dressed that I might have expected for a country doctor, and from his easy entrance, obviously on close terms with the Medinas. He sauntered into the great hall, spied Nicholas and raised a casual hand in greeting. "Ah, Nicholas. Good evening . . ."

Was this the man who had diagnosed my sister's death-illness as "something in the blood"? My suspicions flared forth again, and pushing my chair hastily from the table, I rose to follow Nicholas into the hall.

"How are you, old friend?" said Dr. Leon, grasping Nicholas' chin with a practised hand and turning his head this way and that for observation. "Ah—pale! Slept badly, have you? Lack of appetite?"

"We have a visitor, Charles." My brother-in-law sketched an apology for a smile, and it was evident his undertone had surprised the doctor.

"Oh?" said Dr. Leon, recovering himself. "But that is splendid, splendid! Exactly what you need."

He made to move onward toward the supper room, but Nicholas stood in front of him. "It is Elizabeth's brother," he said in a half-whisper, and Dr. Leon halted quickly.

"Ah?" he said, newly surprised. "You mean he has . . ." Then his quick eyes, peering around the great height of Nicholas, spied me standing in the doorway. "Ah, there he is," he added, and with a wide smile of welcome, he came toward me before Nicholas could restrain him.

"Dr. Charles Leon, at your service, sir," he said, extending his hand. "You are, I understand, Elizabeth's brother?"

I touched his hand briefly, said "Doctor Leon," with a curt bow. Who and what was Doctor Charles Leon the he might use my sister's given name so freely or expect his hand to be accepted by a gentleman? From the uneasy smile of my brother-in-law who had come up beside us, I thought he was well aware of my distaste, but Dr. Leon himself seemed perfectly at home.

"Yes, yes!" he was saying, peering at me closely. "The resemblance is clear—the coloring, the configuration. Beautiful woman, your sister. Perfectly stunning!"

Quickly, I looked at Nicholas Medina; his expression was uneasy, but expressed none of the reactions I would have expected to such familiarity from one who was no more than an upper-class servant. Instead, he seemed quite willing that Dr. Leon should usher himself into the supper room without further ado, and bustle for ward to bow over Catherine Medina's hand.

"My dear," he said, "I see I've interrupted your meal. Ah well," with a casual shrug, "proper timing never was my forte."

I thought Catherine's smile and bow caused her some effort, but Nicholas was nervously hospitable. "Maximilian, another place at table," he ordered. "Come in, Charles; join us."

"Only a glass for me," Dr. Leon interrupted.

"You've already dined?"

"Yes, yes," the doctor said vigorously, "somewhere along my way—I forget exactly where." Seating himself in the great carved chair Maximilian had placed neatly between Dona Catherine and myself at the side of the long supper table, Charles Leon sought to include me in his high spirited conversation.

"A doctor's life, you know, Mr. Bernard—one must crowd in the little essentials of sustenance wherever possible! Food, sleep, conversation—a doctor is lucky to have any time at all for them." He turned to Nicholas easily, "I just happened to be passing by, returning from Baztan. A child delivery. Dona Liana—*twins,* b'Our lady!"

Nicholas and I had resumed our seats at the table, while Maximilian filled the goblet before Dr. Leon with the same excellent golden wine we had had with dinner. It was evidently no stranger to the man; he chuckled gently, smacked hi slips, and raised the glass in a casual salute to Dona Catherine. Then he downed more than half the liquid at one gulp.

We ate in silence until he had set down the glass. "So, young gentleman," he said to me, "you're come all the way from England, have you?" I nodded brusquely, and he maundered on, "Terrible tragedy, your sister's death. Appalling business!"

"How are things in Baztan, Charles?" Nicholas inserted nervously.

Dr. Leon was easily deflected. "What—in Baztan? Oh, as always, Nicholas. As always. Buying and selling, living and dying . . . the warp and wolf of Life . . ." He raised his hand to drain the wine goblet, none to steadily, I suddenly noticed; unquestionably it was not the first refreshment Dr. Leon had had that evening. *In vino veritas,* they say—and I had an idea I might learn more from the doctor now than when he was fully in command of himself.

Leaning forward, I fixed him with a pleasant smile, and asked "*Why did my sister die, Dr. Leon?*"

There was a moment of stricken silence about the table. Dr. Leon uttered a curious heavy grunt, but his gaze met mine squarely. "Have you not been told?"

"Yes, of course he has," Nicholas said hastily.

"Well, then . . ." Charles Leon shrugged casually and abandoned the subject, reaching for the wine decanter to refill his goblet generously. Beyond him, I could see Catherine's face, rigidly averted and frozen in apprehension, her breath held taut.

"I should like to hear the complete story, *from you,* Dr. Leon," I said compellingly.

The doctor took a brief sip of wine. "Her—death was inevitable, I fear, under the circumstances. This castle, this odious atmosphere—"

"What has the castle to do . . ." he repeated, in evident surprise. Turning to Nicholas, he said, "I thought you had *told* him—"

"Now I will have the truth! How did Elizabeth die?"

Dr. Leon glanced once more at my brother-in-law, who only sighed. "It is too late, Charles." Covering his forehead with one hand, he added sadly, "I didn't want him to know. . . ."

"Know *what?*"

"Your sister's death was caused by failure of the heart, sir, due to total shock," Dr. :eon told me with sudden formality. "Literally, she died of fright."

Slowly I digested his words, looking from one face to another. Catherine's eyes fell before my gaze; Nicholas sat, ashen-faced, boneless as a whipped dog, and only the heavy arm of his chair held him from total collapse.

"Why did you not tell me this? I raged, but he only shook his head, struggling to form words with trembling lips.

"I—thought to spare you, sir," he muttered.

"You thought to *deceive* me!"

"No," Catherine protested sharply. "That is untrue, Mr. Barnard." Her eyes met mine forcefully. "Are you the happier for your knowledge?" she asked bitterly, nodding slightly toward Nicholas Medina's unhappy figure.

"What is all this conversation?" Dr. Leon inquired, and, in truth, he did sound bewildered. But I was in no mood to believe anything from anyone, now. From the very first moment of my entrance into Castle Medina I had received nothing but unfriendly silence and, when I'd finally forced an issue, lies.

I could well believe that my sister might have died of "fright." But before we were through, I meant to know exactly what *kind* of fright . . . for the bold little Elizabeth I remember was not of a temper to swoon away in a fit of the vapors. What had this Nicholas Medina done to her in his exquisite chambers "furnished with dedicated love"?

Deliberately I moved toward my brother-in-law and said, "What happened, Don Medina—where and how?

He stared at me, haunted by unknown horror, but I bent him to my will. "*Show me . . .*"

With a shuddering sigh, he capitulated. "Very well, Mr. Barnard," and his voice was a mere whisper.

From the opposite end of the supper table, Catherine Medina sprang erect and came swiftly to stand beside her brother. "No, Nicholas. . . ."

"Hiding him behind a petticoat, Dona Medina?" I said.

She straightened like a coiled spring suddenly released and spat at me with blazing eyes, "No—he is not well enough. I should have thought any dolt could see as much!"

"There is no other way, my dear," Nicholas told her gently. "We were very wrong to have kept it from Mr. Barnard." Pulling himself slowly from his chair, he muttered, "Now we are doubly suspect in his eyes. . . ."

"Suspect?" Dr. Leon's voice was startled. "Suspected of *what,* Nicholas?"

I looked at the man and considered many things: such as the fact that he might, or might *not,* really be a doctor . . . or that if he were, he might easily find a potion to stop my inconvenient questions. But I knew at all costs, even if it meant my life, I had to go on.

Firmly I walked to the door of the dining salon, and turned. "I will follow you, sir," I said to Nicholas, and like a mesmerized mare, he moved slowly toward me.

"Nicholas!" Dr. Leon said sternly, and my brother-in-law hesitated, half-turned. You should *not* be doing this! You know my warnings!"

Nicholas shrugged slightly. "It cannot be avoided," he said fatalistically,
and continued his slow progress toward me. At the door he bowed to me, and such is the training of an aristocrat, he gestured that I should precede.

I, too, possess the courtesies of good family/ "I will follow you, sir." For a second our eyes met and clashed.

Head erect, Nicholas Medina led the way; Catherine and Dr. Leon brought up the rear of our procession.

But what was I to be shown?

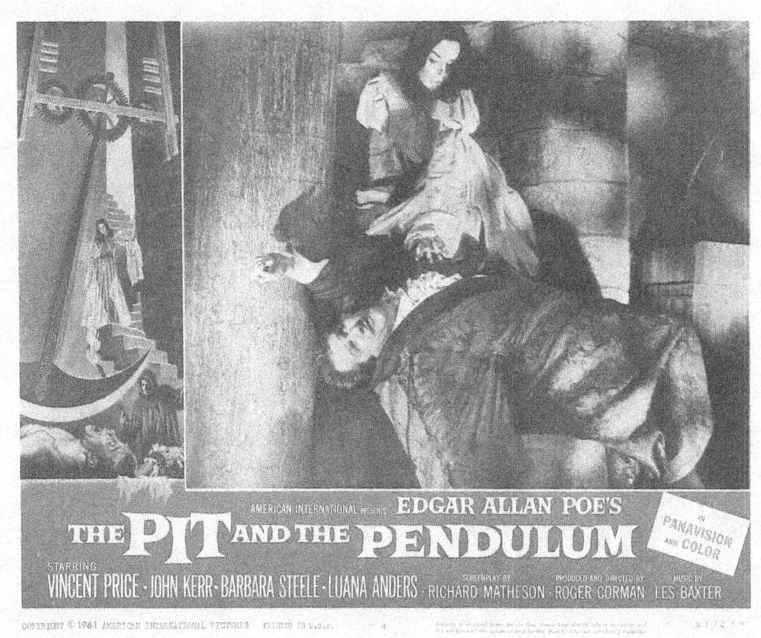

CHAPTER SEVEN

WITHOUT words, we made out way across the great entrance hall to the narrow stairway I had been shown to before with Dona Catherine. Once more, I traversed the echoing stones of the lower corridor following the tall figure of Don Medina. The flickering torches against the corridor walls made a monster of his shadow.

His pace quickened as we turned into that same side passage in which I had first encountered him. He seemed, here, to feel on accustomed ground. Extending his long arm, he picked a torch from the wall with a casual motion, and moved toward the forbidding door that barred our way. At last, we were only steps from the heavy wood, and he stopped so abruptly that I had nearly over-run him.

Passing his hand over his forehead, he appeared suddenly to be conscious of where we were, and he turned to direct over his shoulder a dazed and uneasy gaze at his followers. For a moment, I thought he would refuse to go farther, but with a memory of that Hellish noise I had heard previously, I was determined to proceed.

"Well?" I said coldly. "Why do we stop?"

Bracing himself, Nicholas took the key from his pocket and once more hesitated with a half-pleading glance, but I merely took a step forward and waited. With a deep breath, he turned to unlock the door and push it open. Slowly, creakingly, it swung wide, and I moved forward, forcing Nicholas to precede me, and aware of the tension in Catherine and Dr. Leon who walked behind me.

I stepped over the threshold, and found myself in a gigantic, high-ceilinged chamber that seemed partly cut from living rock. Narrow, barred windows slit the opposite walls, and cold, after the storm, moonlight illumined the place.

Beyond, I could faintly hear the booming surf of the ocean surrounding the promontory of Castle Medina

It was a dank and unwholesome spot, evidently well below the land-level of the castle, for every now and then a froth of spray heaved up from the ocean tossed itself through the window slits. I could well believe many Medinas must have died of the ague in the centuries since the place was built.

In the light of my brother-in-law's flickering torch, I saw that we stood on a balcony without a parapet; a flight of steps curved from one end, twisting itself about a stone pillar to descend into the room below. Nicholas moved to the edge of the balcony; I moved beside him, and together we looked down—upon horror unimaginable.

Slowly my eyes swept about, absorbing the significance of the strange objects placed below. None of them had I ever glimpsed before, and now—in an eerie combination of moonlight and torch flames, covered with dust and cobwebs—it was some moments before I recognized the vileness that confronted me.

Yet—surely I was not mistaken? That hideous shape, with its door swung back to expose spikes within, could only be the famous "Iron Maiden"; those metal bars fixed against the stone wall, with rope leading to a saw toothed wooden wheel—that was a torture rack!

With mounting nausea, I gazed from one to another of the objects: in a corner, the bed of weed hewn to the length of a man but furnished with a mattress of sharp nails; beside it, on the floor, an unmistakable "Iron Boot"—and on both walls, an open hearth that could only have been used for heating pokers, pincers, gouges. . . .

Retreating a pace, I turned to face Nicholas Medina, and in a voice I could scarcely control, I stated, rather than asked, "A *torture chamber!*"

He winced as my voice echoed from the stone surrounding us. "My—father's," he nodded. And as long last my mind created a connection. The portrait in my room, its somber garb. . . .

"Sebastian Medina!" I said, and could not restrain the sick horror in my bones. One of the most infamous, degraded, assistants to the Grand Inquisitor Torquemada—who was, himself, an assistant to the Devil!"

"*Enough,* sir, I beg of you! he pleaded, and Catherine Medina protested, "Mr. Barnard, can you not *see* that . . ."

I could, I thought, begin to see far too much. "*What was my sister doing down here?*"

Nicholas averted his head and Dr. Leon spoke loudly, "I must caution you sir. . . ." But I was beyond consideration for anyone. Was it possible that Nicholas Medina had . . .

"Why was my sister ever *shown* this place? What was she *doing* here?" I shouted.

"She could not keep herself away," Nicholas whispered, and moved unsteadily toward the staircase.

We descended, as before, with Nicholas Medina leading the way, and Dona Catherine and the doctor following me. Nicholas set his torch into a wall bracket, and as he turned, I caught his arm in a firm grip, forcing him to face me. "That *noise* I heard when I was down here earlier . . . is that what—?"

"No, no," he said quickly. "That—device was not in operation at the time."

I looked about me at the hellish instruments, and it was true they seemed all rusted, long out of use. "*Which* device?"

He gestured slightly, and I noted another heavy door, closed and bolted, leading away from beneath the balcony. "In the adjoining chamber, sir," he said. "It play no part—please, let us not discuss it. . . ."

Still I grasped his arm in hands made strong by mingled terror and rage. "The story, sir," I reminded him. "In every detail. . . .*I will have the story!*"

He looked at me strangely, almost with non-recognition, then his glance moved away, raking the room in which we stood. "This was my father's world, Mr. Barnard," he said at last. "A world of pain—bestial cruelty.

"You were right, Sebastian Medina *was* degraded . . . mad . . . inflicting physical agony was his only object in life." Nicholas shuddered under my grasp, and groaned. "The shrieking of mutilated victims was the only music his ears could enjoy."

Slowly my hands released him and he slumped back against the slimy damp walls, as Catherine and Dr. Leon came swiftly forward.

"Nicholas," she pleaded, "Don't—"

"At least spare yourself this, Nicholas," Dr. Leon added.

"Was he not my father? Am I not the spawn of his depraved blood?"

"His depravity is not yours, Nicholas!" Catherine said urgently. "Why scourge yourself because of it?"

"You have not answered me, Don Medina!" I interrupted bluntly. "The story of my sister's death, if you please . . ."

"Yes," he agreed. "I will not dwell upon the history of this blasphemous chamber. Suffice to say that the blood of a thousand men and women has been spilled within its walls. Limbs have been twisted and broken—" Catherine caught her breath in a sob, but he ignored her. "—eyes were gouged from bleeding sockets . . . flash burned black—"

With an effort I held my mind from the fancies his words depicted. "Why do you tell me these things? What have they to do with *my sister?*"

He looked about him and murmured, as if to himself, "I should never have brought her to this place. She was too sensitive, too aware. . ."

"Aware of *what?*" I insisted.

"Of the malignant atmosphere within this castle," he told me. "You have demanded the truth, Mr. Barnard? That is it. Castle Medina destroyed her."

I looked at him increduously, recalling the arrogant beauty of the girl whose portrait hung above-stairs. "My sister was a strong and willful woman, and not one subject to the influence of . . . atmosphere!"

"You have been within this castle for only hours, Mr. Barnard," he replied. "You cannot visualize what it is like to live here month after month, year upon year, breathing its infernal air, absorbing the miasma of barbarity which permeates its walls, particularly—this chamber."

Surprisingly, his voice strengthened slightly and he continued almost matter-of-factly, "It did not bother her, either . . . at first. Our life was *good*, rich with the shared pleasures of our love.

"I delighted to wait upon her. I determined that my hands alone should serve my adored one. Each morning it was I who took the breakfast tray from Maria in the hall and brought it to our bed. It was I who drew back the bed curtains, who woke her with a kiss, who received the first sleepy smile of her day.

"No eyes but mine ever saw the pure alabaster of her shoulder, with the silken night-robe slipping aside," Nicholas said dreamily. "It was I who poured out the posset of new milk, who prepared the fresh egg—and often fed it to her, spoonful by spoonful . . .

"Each morning we rode together," Turning to me, he remarked conversationally, "She was a superb horsewoman; I think it is only the English who have such understanding, such union, with a horse. I bought her a sweet little mare, an Arab filly with a tender mouth and cunning tricks. But my lovely one was equal to all of them!

"We would ride into the countryside and dismount, to sit together on a flowery bank and bask in the quiet of Nature." His voice trailed away, and he looked, smilingly, into a past no one could share. "Sometimes," he said gently, "she would sing for me . . . your English tunes, with certain French airs she'd learned from her aunt. Her voice held a purity . . . she never needed accompaniment, believe me, sir. . . ."

Unwillingly, I relaxed; his voice cast such a spell over me. I could fancy and even believe in his love for a beautiful young wife. Despite the foul chamber in which we stood, I could picture a happiness that made my heart ache. Would I ever find a woman to give me what my sister had given to Nicholas Medina?

"In the afternoon, she usually sat for me while I attempted to capture her beauty on canvas," Nicholas continued. "I did that portrait which you saw in her room, but it was only one of a dozen, and although it is the best, it is all inadequate to recall the loveliness of her."

Unconsciously, my interest quickened. Nicholas Medina had done that picture? He was an artist of no mean ability, then, and I felt sure his capacity for capturing a likeness would have been vastly pleasing to Elizabeth. She had ever a liking to be center of attention.

"We dined together," he was saying. "Never did I shut away her beauty from my salon; never did I receive those who might have been offensive to her, nor entertain anyone unsuited to her acquaintance. Never did I bid her keep to her own quarters.

"Sometimes we dined alone, and enjoyed intimate conversation over the finest dishes. You must know that I procured a masterly cook from Paris for her special pleasure!" he told me in a fleeting aside. "In wines and foods, her palate was perfect!

"Occasionally, there were guest—Dr. Leon, perhaps." Nicholas smiled reflectively. "Charles had ever a ready wit to delight my darling with his tales of the countryside. Later, she played for me, each evening, and for her sake, my agents scoured Paris, Milan, Madrid, to obtain the newest music."

He paused with a slight frown then smiled tenderly. "I had cause to admonish her over only one fault," he told me confidentially. "She *would* forget her ring, leaving it behind her on the harpsichord when she rose to rejoin us! Ah, how many times I have picked it up—and kissed it again onto her hand!

Elizabeth would have liked that, I thought silently.

"Life was simple, quiet, richly pleasurable," he went on, "and then—" his voice trembled, "then the darkness began to fall. . . ."

The Pit and the Pendulum

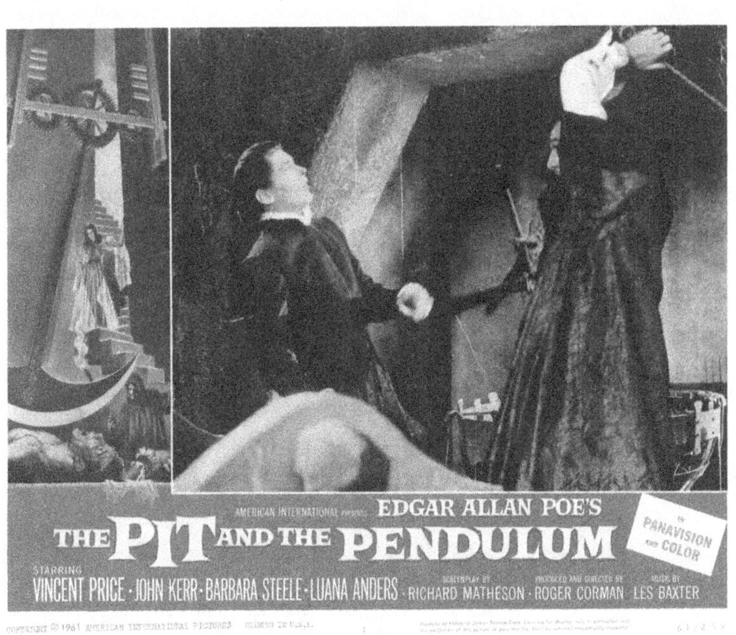

CHAPTER EIGHT

AS IF his words had brought eclipse, the moonlight suddenly vanished behind clouds. Released from the spell of Nicholas Medina's vibrant voice, I came once more to myself. Still we stood in the dank stone room, surrounded by horrible devices of torture—and still I knew neither *why* nor *how* my sister should have died.

In the uneasiness betrayed by Catherine and Dr. Leon's faces, my suspicions revived, and I realized that for all of the wonderful words, the heartbreaking sadness, of answers, I had *none.* Angered by my own weak emotional response that had nearly lulled me to forgetfulness of my purpose, I snapped, "What darkness, sir?"

"The darkness of a clouded mind, sir," Nicholas said in faint surprise.

His words struck me cold as the ocean spray dashing up behind us. Did the man mean to imply that Elizabeth was of unsound intellect? If so, God damn him for a Spanish trickster, and a length of steel would quickly show him there was at least one Barnard to defend Elizabeth's honor. . . . But even as my hand flew to the Toledo dagger at my belt, he continued his story.

"More and more, upon entering her room in the mornings, I would find her awake, and discover that she had not slept all the night, she did not know why. I laid down more carpets about the halls and chambers, forbade the servants to enter her wing until mid-day and banished the gardeners who might have disturbed her rest by panting and pruning without. . . . But it did not answer. Still she lay awake. . . .

"Her appetite began to fade. No longer did she savor any dish; she began to lose weight and her cheeks paled. When I coaxed her to eat, the food she had formerly enjoyed only made her sick.

She walked in her sleep," he went on brokenly. "I would come upon her wandering the corridors at night. I tried—dear God, how I tried—to find what was wrong, but she had never an answer . . . except to say that *something* was oppressing her."

With a groan, he turned his head from side to side in evident agony. "God and Sweet Mary help me for my blindness! I should have known, *I should have known. . . .*" Controlling himself with an effort, he said, "One day, she disappeared. Frantic, I searched the castle for her. She was nowhere above-stairs, and at last I came below, thinking she might have taken a fancy to visit the wine cellars or the pantry. You understand?

“”Passing along the corridor, I turned, and saw this door standing open.” His voice sank with remembered anguish. “Yes—Elizabeth was within! As I stood on the balcony, transfixed with horror, I could see her adorable figure below me. She was wandering about, the silken hem of her gown bedraggled and torn by the filthy stone floor, leaving the precious stones of her embroidered skirt in tiny pools of light behind her as she moved.

“Then I knew,” said Nicholas Medina—and I shall never hope to hear more sorrow and torment in human voice. “My castle and its awful history had oppressed her . . . these very instruments of torture which were my birthright and *my* curse now cursed *her* as well, infecting her with a kind of haunted fascination.”

I was overcome by horror at his tale. I glanced about me. I thought it must be entirely true—I could envision Elizabeth, beautiful as heaven but fascinated by hell.

My brother-in-law continued. “I watched her drawn from one torture device to another—as if the aura of pain and suffering which surrounded them was luring her to sickness, to madness—to death. . . .

“Oh, I ran down the stairway as quickly as might be . . . I have no real recollection of my descent,” Nicholas sighed, “though from the bruises I discovered later, I must have stumbled badly. But as she turned and saw me, she cried out piteously . . . stretched out her arms, and fell against me.”

His arms reached out in remembered agony. “I bore her up to her chamber,” he told me proudly. “It was my arms alone that held her, laid her gently on her bed, summoned Maria to her assistance. All night I sat beside her bed, holding those fragile fingers and planning a new future for both of us.

“I determined to leave the castle *at once,*” Don Medina went on. “We would travel for a while, restore our spirits. . . .” Remembering, his face lightened briefly. “I thought even to journey into England for a sight of *you,* sir, and at last, we would make our home elsewhere. I would abandon this accursed spot; we would seek an estate of rolling hill and pleasant flowers.

“When she awoke, I told her my decision—and she smiled at me, Mr. Bernard! The smile of an angel! For a week, all was bustle and arrangement, and momentarily, as the hour for our departure grew near, she strengthened and regained color. Once more, we dined sumptuously for the last time in state together in the dining salon—Charles Leon was with us. And then . . .”

He closed his eyes with a shudder once more, then continued with determination, "On the very eve of our departure, as Charles and I sat below over a final glass of wine after my darling had retired, the travelling trunks packed and corded to the coach, and the dressing bags and jewel cases waiting for the last essentials . . . we heard a scream from below . . . the most hideous, blood-chilling scream I have ever heard in my life!"

My brother-in-law's tall body writhed away from us to face the dank stones of the torture chamber, and Catherine slipped about me rapidly, to put her arms around his quivering frame.

"It was a scream of pure terror," Dr. Leon muttered beside me. "I have never heard its like, Mr. Barnard. We sprang from our chairs and we slipped in the wine we had overturned in our haste as we turn to run . . . but we knew not *where.*"

"*I* knew where, Charles—I knew only to well!" Nicholas' voice was muffled, one clenched fist beat against the stone slab.

"Hush!" said Catherine, cradling him in her arms like a baby. "Hush, Nicholas—this is too much blame, more than you deserve."

In the face of the pain of the Medinas and Catherine's reproachful glance, I felt a part of their tragedy. How, I wondered, would *I* have borne such a grim and loathsome heritage?

Yet it had to be ended, and only by a full disclosure of each last dread detail, for Nicholas Medina had known his family and its unsavory history, but had still dared to marry. Into the vile tradition of the Medinas, he had drawn my sister, and innocent, high-spirited girl, born of fine family and reared with every accomplishment befitting a lady. And by that marriage, he had condemned her to Purgatory, if no worse. I could not condone it, and I believed that I might have felt equally as strong had that girl *not* been my own sister. . . .

Hardening my heart, I turned to Dr. Leon. "Continue," I bade him, harshly.

One eye on the shaking form of Don Medina, he complied in an undertone. "We rushed from the hall, and found this door standing wide as you see it now, fir. Within, we saw nothing at first—no sign of movement, or trace of life. Nicholas plunged down the stairs, however, and ran from object to object, while I followed closely. Truly, I feared for his sanity, sir," he told me earnestly.

"As I fear for mine until I know the final truth," I countered coldly.

"Of course," he said hurriedly. "Your emotion is understandable, even admirable sir. . . ."

"And then?"

With a deep breath, he calmed himself and said, baldly, "Very well, if you will have it, sir. We found her in the Iron Box. It was Nicholas who noticed the door was closed, the cobwebs disturbed. The tragedy was all to evident; she had as you have heard developed a morbid interest in this fearful place. Stealing away from her attendants,she had made her way here once more in the sick fancies of her mind and stepping into the—instrument—had somehow managed to close the door upon herself."

Unwillingly my eyes followed the direction of his fore-finger, pointing out to me that hideous object which had encompassed my sister's death. Beside me, Nicholas Medina had drawn himself from his sister's comforting arms. Together we gazed at the box, as Dr. Leon went on, "No words can describe the expression of terror frozen to her lovely face, sir! We tore aside the clasps, pulled away the iron door to receive her unconscious form in our arms.

"My God!" Nicholas whispered, and for a moment thought he would fall to the floor. . . . Yet, as I reached to support him, I caught a glimpse of Dr. Leon's face. He still stared at the box, and incredible as it seemed, I thought there was about his lips a smile of—something akin to pleasure!

Nicholas leaned upon me heavily for a space, and said,"We brought her out of the box; I held her in my arms, Mr. Barnard—just *there* . . ." He gestured. But in my shock, I could only stare at him. "Just before she—died—she whispered a name: *Sebastian.*"

On a sudden, the moon emerged from behind the scudding clouds and its cold beams streamed through the window slits. I turned involuntarily to glance at the furnishings of this hell-hole. Nicholas, too, scanned the place wildly, murmuring *"Sebastian . . . Sebastian. . ."*

Then, before we could move, he had torn away from us and rushed toward the death-box, screaming with all the vigor of his immense frame, *"Sebastian! May Hell take your soul. . . ."*

CHAPTER NINE

I STOOD on a battlement of Castle Medina, which I had discovered beyond one of the long windows to my chamber. The moonlight silvered potted shrubbery and stone alike, and below me the ocean surf beat itself endlessly against the scarp. In a desperate effort to distract and calm my mind, I forced myself to consider what I knew of geography: where did this rolling ocean lead? What lay beyond the moon-path across the heaving water? Was it the land of the Moors—or new lands discovered by the Cabots?

The air was rain-washed by the storm, fresh and clean to my face, slowly bringing peace and clarity. Leaning against the parapet, I found myself relaxing from the tumultuous emotions of the past hours. I had accepted the fact of Elizabeth's death, though I could not yet bear to consider its details. And I thought, too, that the failure of Don Nicholas Medina to notify me formally was also admissible; the torment of his grief was unquestioned.

With inward relief, I decided that the questions that had brought me to Spain were now answered. Elizabeth's modest dowry was certainly insufficient to tempt a man of Medina's wealth—and, however reluctantly, I had

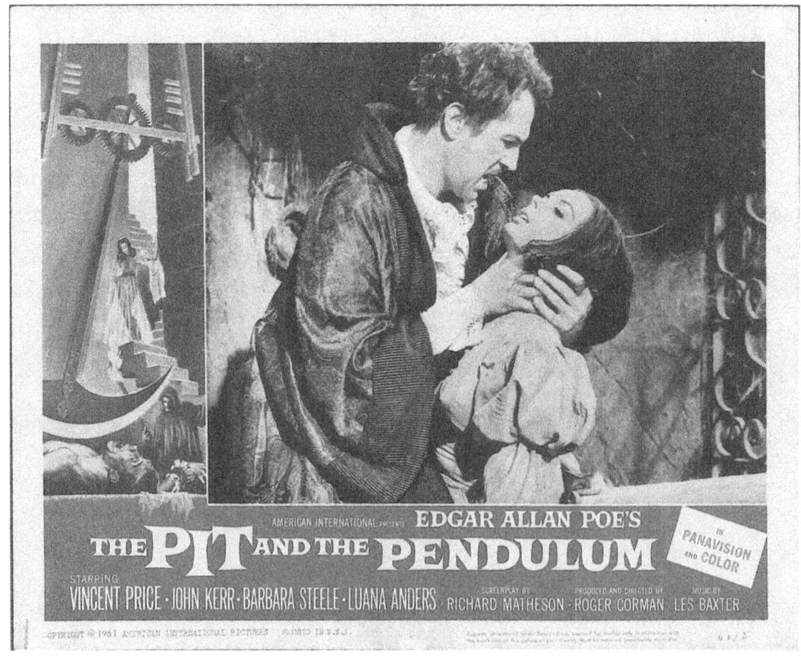

to admit I believed his wild adoration of my sister. Impossible to conceive that he had deliberately caused her death, either to enjoy her money or to supplant her by another woman!

I thought I would forever be unhappy at the memory of her untimely loss, for certainly Elizabeth, judging by her portrait, had been uniquely formed for life and all it might offer. Nor could I justly condemn our aunt for her speedy acceptance of Medina's marriage offer; to her trivial mind, an alliance with a Medina would have seemed beyond anything great! Even had she been aware of it, the unsavory background of the Medinas would have been dismissed with a shrug of the shoulder and the comment, "Oh, it was only the father, after all; every family has its scandals, my dear—and do but consider the wealth, the luxury, the comfort!"

Yes, however I might deplore the facts, I could only admit all seemed explained most fully . . . and certainly at terrible cost to my brother-in-law. I felt sorry that my position as head of our family required me to drive him to a point of collapse—but on the other hand, why had not Catherine or Dr. Leon, averted my visit entirely by sending me a formal letter?

Drily, I thought that if only *someone* had taken this trouble, he might have told me almost *anything* and been spared at least a little of his torment; I was religious enough even by Papist standards to feel certain from what I had heard that for the rest of his life he would pay all, and even more, than I could wish for his share of responsibility in Elizabeth's death. It had not needed me to add to that eternal memory.

But now, at last, I knew what was to be known, and I could set my face toward England once more on the morrow. The thought was good. I wondered how my horses fared, who was exercising them during my absence; I thought of my younger sister Anne, and knew quite certainly that on my return she would have a welcome present for me . . . perhaps a shirt of her own weaving, for she was already a notable artisan although she was only ten. And there was Robert, my prankish youngest brother; there would be sad tales and earnest complaints from the estate agents over his rabbit snares!

I had nearly forgotten how far I was from all the delights of Chipham Manor when a soft voice said, "Mr. Barnard!"

"Yes?" I said, still lost in my dream of home and supposing the voice no more than a servant come to open the bed.

But the voice repeated with soft insistence, "Mr. Barnard, if you please!"

Turning, I was astonished to see Dona Catherine Medina standing hesitantly within my room, and hastily I went toward her. "Dona," I said formally, "forgive me."

"I—took the liberty of entering . . ." she said hurriedly.

"But of course." I assured her, but inwardly all my doubts rose. For an unmarried daughter of a high-born Spanish family to enter a man's bedroom alone and unchaperoned at any hour of the day—let alone full night, as it now was—argued an urgency that over set all my painfully achieved mental balance.

Why had she come, why did she jeopardize her reputation, her whole future . . . to say nothing of her virginity, since I was a young and healthy male, and despite her iron petticoat frame, Catherine Medina possess a definite charm. . . .

"How is your brother?" I asked.

"Better, thank you. Charles—Dr. Leon is with him." She paused, seeming not to know quite what she would say next. Then, "I have come to beg you to please believe him, Mr. Barnard." She extended one hand pleadingly. "I assure you, he has told you the truth."

"Has he?"

"*Yes,*" she said eagerly. "Mr. Barnard, in not telling you before, Nicholas meant only to spare you pain. He is a good man, sir, a kind and gentle man. I know that he adored your sister."

Beneath the heart-shaped stiffened lace of her cap, Catherine's face was earnest, anxious, and I wondered whether her obvious love for and faith in her brother was justified. "I would like to believe him, Dona Medina," I told her.

God knows I meant every word, for I wanted nothing so much as to be satisfied so I might leave this accursed castle!

"But I find it very difficult. There is something about him that I cannot help but sense . . . a kind of fearful tension and—I am sorry to cause you pain—but an air of definite guilt."

"Of *course* he suffers from guilt," she told me, impatiently.

"The memory of our father might be enough to kill any man so sensitive and loving as my brother. When that fact is coupled with the terrible loss of your sister who was his adored wife. . . . *Think* what this must mean, Mr. Barnard!"

She turned from me and took a few steps about the room, as though she were in the grip of emotion too great for her youth and inexperience.

For the first time, I realized she was about my own age, and not ill-favored, if one could but strip away the unflattering Spanish costume. No matter what the outcome of our meeting, I knew Dona Catherine would never have reason to complain of my respect; I could only hope that her visit might be known only to Maria or Maximilian, whom I was certain would never reveal it. But Catherine herself seemed entirely unaware of any indiscretion.

"How shall I convince you?" she murmured, as if to herself. "Perhaps it will help you to understand if I tell you . . ." Swiftly she turned toward me, her hand catching the back of a high carved chair for support, and I saw that she had nerved herself to the last ounce of her strength for an ordeal she conceived to be hideous, yet essential. "It was something that happened when Nicholas was a mere child. Something I have never shared with anyone, Mr. Barnard. But now . . . perhaps it may help. It *must!*"

I walked forward and gently took her hand from the chair, leading her toward the fire. "Dona Catherine," I said quietly, "I will ever be grateful for anything you choose to tell me—but you must tell it to me in comfort, at ease by your fire . . ."

Like a child, she allowed herself to be placed in a chair with a hassock thrust beneath her tiny feet. She sank back with a weary sigh, as I threw another log on the fire and stirred it with the poker to greater exertions. Her face smote me by its pinched unhappiness, and I poured her a glass of the fine wine with which I noticed my decanter had been replenished.

I pulled the long glass door to the battlements partway closed; the fresh air had been grateful to my lungs, and suddenly realized I could not bear the thought that Dona Catherine Medina should suffer either!

She thanked me with a wan smile. I sat down in the chair opposite her by the fire, and said "Now, tell me what you will . . ."

She shivered slightly and fixed her eyes on the fire. "It was a day when Nicholas was a little boy. He was playing in the lower corridor," she began in a low voice. "He had a ball and that was a perfect place for bouncing it, but it rolled beyond him, into the side corridor.

"As children," she continued, "We were strictly forbidden to play there at all . . . but Nicholas was forgetful; the door was ajar, too great a temptation. He had been forbidden by our father, Don Sebastian, to enter that chamber at any time. The curiosity of youth, however, overcame his fear of challenging our father's discipline. He *had* to see what lay beyond the door. . . ."

I could well understand that childish disobedience, yet what a dreadful spectacle for young eyes!

"The—chamber was empty," Dona Catherine went on, "with only a low fire burning in once of the hearths. Nicholas crept quietly down the stairway, the better to examine the strange . . . objects." Catherine's voice grew, faint. "He has described to me his growing sense of evil, Mr. Barnard, as he looked more closely from one to another and realized that the filthy stains were . . . not rust . . . but *dried blood.*

"He was about to run from the place in terror when, suddenly from the balcony above, he heard footsteps and voices approaching. Overcome by fear of discovery and the inevitable punishment if our father caught him, Nicholas hid himself behind—behind . . .*that iron box.*

"From his hiding place, he saw a robed and terrible figure entering the balcony; our father, Don Sebastian Medina."

Involuntarily, I looked up to the portraits above the fireplace.

"Yes," Catherine said, "that is he—but the portrait does not show his limp, nor the nervous tic with which his head was afflicted, Mr. Barnard. On that terrible day, he brought with him our mother, Isabella, and our uncle Bartolome, who was my father's brother . . . and as they stepped forward onto the balcony, Don Sebastian closed and bolted shut the great door behind them.

"All three came down the stairway, and walked about the chamber. At first it appeared that, for some inexplicable reason, our father was actually conducting them on a tour of his ghastly room," she continued. "Nicholas could see that both our mother and uncle were uneasy and frightened. Our father's smiling affability as he described the workings of these hellish instruments turned Nicholas's blood cold.

"The evil he had but half-comprehended in his own short examination was suddenly fully revealed to him, but more than that—as he observed the adults, he sensed a mounting premonition. Even a little boy, no more than seven years of age, he knew something was wrong—most terribly wrong. He sensed it like a darkening vapor in the air . . . because there was no *reason* for our mother and our uncle to have been there.

"And then—" Catherine's voice halted, tried to resume, could only repeat: And then—"

I moved from my chair to hold the wine to her lips. "Rest a while, Dona," I said. "Your distress is too great. I release you from your tale, say no more!"

Gratefully, she sipped the wine. "But I must tell you," she whispered, "so that you can *truly* understand!" Her slender fingers closed about mine, as if to draw strength from them for what was to come.

Setting aside the wine glass, I raised her hand to my lips and gently pressed her icy fingers. "As you will. . . ."

"Our father," she began again, "turned to the hearth fire and removed a white-hot poker. His explanation of its use as a torture sickened the others. My uncle turned away in open disgust—and suddenly, Don Sebastian moved with the speed of a serpent.

"Raising the poker from the glowing coats, he leaped at his brother and struck him to the floor with one terrible blow. Our mother screamed and screamed, as our father beat his only brother to death against the stone slabs."

Catherine's voice was monotonous; she stared unseeing at the fire before us. Her hand gripped mine with feverish intensity, and I sensed she had entered a private world of shock, in which she spoke with understanding, but without reacting to the emotion of what she spoke.

"And all the while, our father shouted one word—again and again: *'Adulterer . . . adulterer!' Nicholas did not even know the* meaning of the word," Catherine murmured. . . ."

"Our mother backed away, her face was a mask of shock and terror. She knew now that our father had lured them there deliberately. And then he turned on *her.*

"He stalked her like a dog in the hunt, Mr. Barnard. . . ."

"No!" I protested. "Say no more, Dona Catherine," but she didn't hear me. Her recital flowed on, well-bred modulations of her monotonous and weary tone.

"He accused her of vile debaucheries with his brother, cursed her as faithless, promised her the agonies of hell in expiation of her infidelity . . .and there, before my brother's very eyes, *our mother was tortured to death."* Catherine had concluded with sobs; her head fell against my shoulder as if near-senseless.

"Hush," I said. "Hush! Think no more on it, Dona. . . ."

She had recovered herself in a moment. "Ever since that day," she said in a more normal tone, "Nicholas has been unable to live as other men. Always, he is haunted by the memory of that terrible scene."

She looked absently into the fire and sighed. "Your sister's death came very close to . . . driving him insane, Mr. Barnard," she told me. "How close, I hesitate to tell you."

Leaning forward, she pleaded earnestly, "I *beg* of you—have pity on him! Help him by believing in him. Your distrust and animosity, together with all these other things might well prove more than he can bear!"

It was my impulse to respond whole-heartedly in sympathy for the nerve-racking ordeal she had voluntarily set herself in relating the horrible history of the Medinas. But an innate caution still restrained me. Catherine Medina's face of innocent hope disturbed me deeply. Did the girl not realize that her dreadful revelation, as well as her desperate plea for my help in averting Nicholas' possible insanity, was capable of *two* interpretations.

For herself, I acquitted *her* totally of any share in Elizabeth's death—

but what of Nicholas and his heritage? *What if he were already insane?*

"I cannot assure you of my total conviction," I told her, trying by a gentle tone to soften the bluntness of my words. "I sympathize with your concern for your brother, Dona Catherine, and I will *try* to believe."

Impulsively, we clasped hands and smiled at each other—then suddenly her eyes widened and she released her hand tremulously, with a furtive glance about the room. I was conscious of inner tender amusement: the child (she was no more than 19, I felt certain) had suddenly realized her presence in a man's bedchamber and was seeking some graceful way to depart as rapidly as might be, short of outright flight!

Formally, I stepped backward and bowed. "I shall forever be grateful for your courage in relating your story to me, Dona."

"Yes, I thank you, sir" she returned hastily. "I must apologize for the intrusion. . . ." She moved a few paces toward the door, "I fear you were tired by your journey, and I have detained you from sleep." She had nearly made her escape, and with two rapid strides I had reached her side to hold open the door politely, as if this were all the most natural occurrence in the world. She drew in her breath with a gasp, dropped me a curtsey, her eyes downcast and murmured, "Goodnight, Mr. Barnard—and thank you!"

"Dona!" I said—but she was gone, melting into the shadows of the corridor, her steps silenced by carpets.

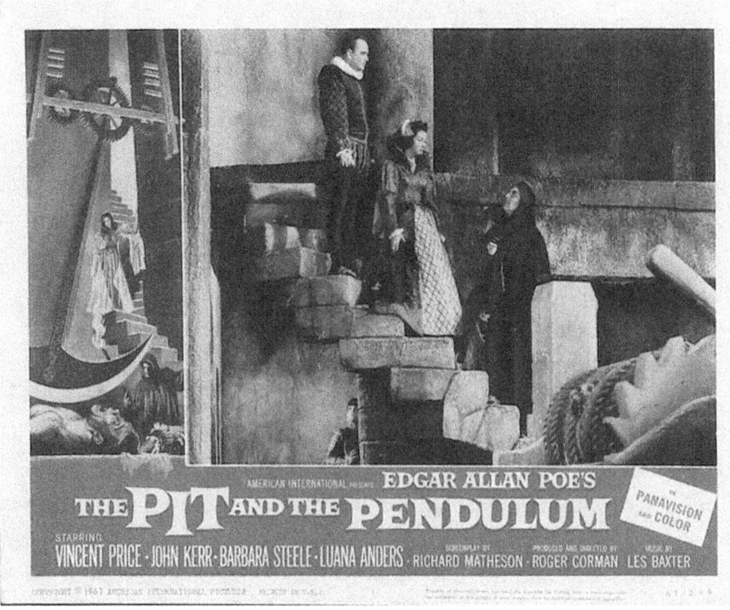

CHAPTER TEN

DESPITE the fact that I had much to recall and digest of the hours since my arrival at Castle Medina, the rigors of my travel and the excellent softness of my bed sent me off to sleep before I had more than scratched the surface of my deliberations.

How long I slept, I do not know. But the fire had burned to a bed if glowing embers half-lost among ashes, and the moon had long since passed her peak when I awoke with a sense of some sound my dreams could not accept as ordinary. Starting from my pillow, my first thought was for an intruder, but the painted chair I had quietly placed beneath my door handle was still in place, and I felt no alien presence beside me.

Then what had awakened me? For a moment I sat still, and in the dim silence of the room I heard faint sounds of a harpsichord. The tune sounded strangely archaic and discordant to my ears, though I am not well-versed in the art.

I do not know what brought me from my bed, to throw about me a night-robe and make my way to the door. Certainly, whatever the hour, it was no concern of mine, and all of a piece with the oddities I had already encountered in Castle Medina, that someone should be playing a harpsichord while normal householders would be asleep.

Nevertheless, I set aside the chair and quietly swung open my door, moving into the corridor. The sound of the harpsichord was clearly rising from below, and something in its wild tunelessness made me uneasy. I moved in the direction of the music, hesitated to listen once more—and a hand fell on my arm!

Whirling with a pounding heart, I saw it was Catherine Medina, wrapped in softest black velvet and quite indistinguishable from the night-shadows but for her ashen white face and terrified eyes. "*Who is it?*" she whispered.

Feeling the delicate Toledo blade my hand had taken almost unconsciously from beneath my pillow, I felt equipped for any human intruder. But what guarantee had I that the musician below was of *this* world? Summoning all my courage, I whispered, "I will see," and moved toward the stairs.

She came up beside me again, catching my arm and breathing "Wait!"

and together we stood, shivering, while the music jangled and crashed from below.

Suddenly, a door jerked open behind us and light fell across the corridor. Half-asleep, still dressed in rumpled clothes, Dr. Leon demanded "Where is Nicholas?"

Catherine stepped toward him quietly. "He's gone from his room?"

"I must have dozed off in my chair," he said with groggy defensiveness against the accusation in her tone. "Then I heard. . . ." With the strange ability of all doctors, he was instantly fully awake; reaching backward into the room, he picked up a taper and moved with stolid determination to the stairs.

"I don't understand," I said in bewilderment to Catherine. "Why are you all so alarmed merely because chooses to play the harpsichord at night?"

She had dropped her grasp of my arm and moved swiftly after Dr. Leon. Looking back at me blindly, she said "No, you don't understand—*Nicholas has never played a harpsichord in his life!*" Then she was gliding down the steps, and after a minute, I followed her . . . but as we heard the bottom of the stairs, the music ceased abruptly/

We froze to our places briefly, but all was impenetrable silence. With a catlike step, Dr. Leon reached up to illumine a wall flambeau and strode across to the music room—then stopped, his taper held high.

It illumined the whimpering figure of Maria, cowering beside the closed door. "I heard the playing," she moaned,"and it frightened me. . . ."

"Go back to bed, child," Dr. Leon said gently, and turned her toward the servants' quarters. Stumbling, she crept away, and we turned to the music room . . .to be stopped again by Catherine's gasp, "*Nicholas!*"

My brother-in-law stood in the shadows of the great hall, pressed against the wall. The flickering flambeau showed him wide-eyes, and expression of mindless horror on his face. "It was Elizabeth," he muttered.

"You *saw* her?" Dr. Leon inquired, aghast.

Nicholas shook his head weakly. "I did not have to see her. I know it was her playing—I would know her touch anywhere."

With a surge of mingled dread and anger, I reached around the doctor to grasp and turn the door handle, and with a mighty heave, pushed it crashing back against the wall.

The room was completely empty.

In the long slanting beams of the settling moon, the harpsichord stood silent and unattended, but its bench was askew, as if from the rapid departure of a performer.

Curiously, I ran from one to another of the long windows.

"Unlocked?" Dr. Leon asked quietly.

"No," I said. "Is there another door?"

"There is not, sir," he said huskily, and turned to his patient.

Nicholas approached, stumbling, timidly holding Catherine's arm. He looked about the room fearfully, as the moonlight was obscured by clouds, and made his way slowly toward the harpsichord. It was a beautiful instrument, even finer than the one I had glimpsed in Elizabeth's sitting room above-stairs. Then, of a sudden, the moon shone forth once more. And Nicholas uttered a great cry of agony.

Gleaming and unmistakable in the silvery light, *Elizabeth's ring lay upon the music stand. . . .*

With an effort, I conquered the chill that suffused me. I went forward and took the ring into my hand. There was no question about it; it was no cunning replica. This was the pictured ring of the portrait, and as I turned it this way and that, its great emerald and matched diamond darted lustrous fire of green and white across the encircling pearls.

After a moment I laid it upon my open palm and extended it toward Don Medina. "This is hers?"

He shrank from me with a whine of pure terror, and seemed to crumple before my eyes. Dr. Leon caught him handily, but the weight of Nicholas's great height might still have carried him to the floor despite the young doctor's strength.

"Easy, Easy, Dr. Leon aid and turned to me urgently, "Your arm, sir!"

For the second time in that hellish night, we supported Nicholas Medina slowly up the stairs to his bedchamber and laid him upon the fine-woven coverlet. Dr. Leon bustled for his remedies, while my brother-in-law twisted in anguish and moaned. All my distaste for the man returned and I would have stepped away but that he caught my arm in a vise-like grip and held me beside him.

"It was she," he confided, feebly. *"It was she!"*

"Don't be absurd, Nicholas," Dr. Leon's voice inserted briskly as he poured and stirred rapidly. "Of course it wasn't."

"Yes," Nicholas insisted weakly, but the doctor was beside us with the potion.

"Nonsense," he said smiling heartiness. "Now, drink this like a brave fellow, and tomorrow things will look clearer."

Between us, with my support to his gaunt shoulders and Dr. Leon's assistance in holding the goblet, Nicholas downed the draft and lay back exhaustedly, his eyes closed. "He'll be asleep in a minute," the doctor said in a professional undertone. "I'll stay beside him until the drug takes effect."

Thus politely dismissed, I turned to the door. In spite of myself, I was impressed by the doctor's quiet competence as he packed his nostrums away neatly in the bag, and rinsed out the goblet with fresh water from the great gold pitcher.

Picking up a taper from the table beside the door, I stepped out into the corridor and became conscious of something still clutched in my hand. Unclenching my fingers, I looked down at it stupidly, then reached my taper upward to light the flambeau above.

It was the ring from the music stand, winking and sparkling at me in the torchlight.

But was it *the* ring?

Nicholas, Catherine, Mr. Barnard and Dr. Leon about to exhume Elizabeth's coffin

CHAPTER ELEVEN

AS I stared and wondered, Catherine came softly up to me. I held out my palm. "Hers?"

Wordlessly, she took the thing into her own slim fingers and examined it carefully. Finally she returned it with a frightened nod just as Dr. Leon left Nicholas' chamber, closing the door quietly behind him.

"He will sleep until morning," he told us.

"But you will stay?" Catherine asked anxiously.

"Of course, my dear! Until daylight, and the time for starting my rounds, at any rate." He patted her arm soothingly, but his eyes strayed to the jewel in my hand. I held it out; he bent for one quick look and muttered shakily, "Oh, my dear Lord!"

"It *is* hers, isn't it? Catherine asked.

"It is," he affirmed, grimly. "But—*how?* Wasn't it on her finger when she was. . . ."

"Yes," he interrupted, "Yes, God knows; *yes.*" He hesitated then said, "I—perhaps I had better tell both of you now. . . ."

"Tell us *what?*" I demanded.

He gestured vaguely. "Not here—perhaps, in your room, sir?"

"Certainly." Once more I had visitors, once more I built up the fire and filled wine glasses, Catherine would have refused hers, but the doctor insisted.

Take it," he said. "Drink every drop. That's a prescription!"

Slowly she obeyed and leaned back in her chair, so white and weary that I felt angered anew. What had ghosts and haunts, spectres or a family curse to do with *her,* poor girl!

"What I am about to tell you, no one in this world but Nicholas and myself know," Dr. Leon said reluctantly. "That is, I had thought no one else knew. . . ." he paused thoughtfully, then continued, "At any rate—to be completely blunt about it—Nicholas believes Elizabeth may have been entombed prematurely."

Any last vestige of sleepiness left me at once! "*What!*" I shouted.

"Oh *no!*" Catherine whispered.

Dr. Leon held up a warning hand. "I hasten to assure you both that such is *not* the case," he said quietly. "Elizabeth was quite dead. I would stake my reputation on that fact."

"Then—"

"Why does Nicholas believe it?" Dr. Leon went on. "Because of what happened to his mother many years ago."

"I am sorry; I do not understand," I said.

"I have told Mr. Barnard what Nicholas saw that day," Catherine added.

"*You* have told . . ." Dr. Leon looked at her in concern. "My dear child, the strain. . . ." He shook his head in distress.

"And what have you to tell us now?" I demanded.

Bracing himself, he spoke to Catherine. "No my dear, your mother was not tortured to death as you were told."

She looked at him bewildered. "But—"

"I know," he said. "She *was* tortured, yes. But—*not to death.* Do I make myself clear?"

Blindly, Catherine reached out her hand; I clasped and held it, and together we stared at the man in sick horror.

"You mother was walled up in her tomb while yet alive."

"*No!* Oh no. . . ."

"From that day forth, the very thought of premature internment was enough to drive your brother into convulsions of horror. As the years went by, it became the one abiding dread of his life," Dr. Leon said evenly. "Something he never mentioned even to you, Catherine."

"It was a dread which sprang forth from its pit of latency after Elizabeth's death and entombment. Nicholas broods about it constantly," he shook his head anxiously, "that I fear for his mind—for the one additional stroke of terror that might . . ." The slight gesture of his hand, describing a graphic curve downward, was brutally frank.

"Already, he has told me that he has—heard her walking in the corridors, heard her voice speaking his name . . . and tonight—" he sighed and shrugged.

Catherine wept. I tried to collect my scattered wits and recollections. "Dr. Leon," I said bluntly.

"Sir?"

"You seem to forget that we *all* heard the harpsichord being played."

"I have not forgotten it, sir. It is why I said before that I had thought only Nicholas and I were in possession of this tale."

He looked at me, as if pitying my slow intellect. "Someone, I fear, has discovered Nicholas' secret fear," he explained carefully, "and is using it to terrible advantage. It might be a servant."

"They are all completely loyal to my brother," Catherine protested.

"I know, I know," the doctor murmured.

"I could—almost more easily believe that . . ." Catherine broke off, shaking her head.

"That *what?*" he inserted sharply.

"Nothing," she said. "I spoke without thought."

What had she started to say, I wondered? But her face, turned sadly toward the fire, gave me no clue. I turned to the doctor and spoke sternly. "I wish to know one thing—*precisely.*" A shade of apprehension passed across his face, then he bowed courteously.

"What you will, sir."

"Are you absolutely positive that Don Medina's dread is unwarranted?"

Catherine's eyes turned to me in shock, and Dr. Leon straightened as though I had pierced him with a knife. "Mr. Barnard! he protested; then, controlling himself, he held my eyes squarely. "Your sister was dead, sir. *Dead.*"

Catherine sank back in her chair with a sigh, and Dr. Leon continued, "If Elizabeth Medina walks the corridors of this castle, it is her *spirit*—not her living self.

"And do you believe in ghosts, Dr. Leon?" I asked softly.

He looked at me, startled. "I fail to understand you, Mr. Barnard."

Deliberately, I placed my hand upon the fire-mantel, leaning easily, smiling casually, as though all were of the utmost normalcy. *"Ghosts,* Dr. Leon," I returned placidly. "Spectres, revenants, ghastly visitors from the nether worlds exacting vengeance or—seeking peace from torment. . . ."

With my final words, my smile vanished; I leaned forward with all the menace at my command—and was rewarded when his face paled, his eyes grew hunted and slid away from mine.

"No," he muttered. "You understood me, Mr. Barnard . . . there is no question of torment—aside from the torment of a mind saddened, weakened. . . ."

But that did not explain, I thought, *Nicholas Medina's anguished plea to his wife's portrait: 'For God's Sweet Sake, Elizabeth, be at peace!'"*

CHAPTER TWELVE

BY MY sensing, it was full eight of the clock when my eyes opened once more to encompass a gloomy sunless day. Hastily springing from my bed, I removed the painted chair that had formed my protection against the lack of key or bolt during the night. I had had a moment's fear lest some servant had tried to enter with my breakfast before I awoke, although after the disturbed and horrifying revelations of the night, I know not why I should have felt apologetic for my barricade!

Nevertheless, I made all speed with my dressing, and in truth, to one who commonly eats at 6 in the morning, a stomach can grow painfully empty by 8! I could only trust there would be food below, and emerging from my room I had started down the corridor toward the staircase when I overheard voices.

The came from a room whose door stood half-ajar, and I heard Catherine's voice.

"I know I should not say it, doctor, but I wish—*God, how I wish*—my brother had never even glimpsed Elizabeth!"

"Now, now," Dr. Leon's voice spoke soothingly. "I don't believe you really mean that, Catherine. You speak rather from distress . . . and quite naturally, quite naturally." I could visualize the doctor's nodding head, that hand patting Dona Catherine's arm. Involuntarily I moved as quietly as possible, to stand beside the door.

"Of course, *now* you feeling is a deep desire that Nicholas had never met a woman whose death could so desolate his life," Dr. Leon went on. "But remember that while she lived, he had the supreme happiness of earthly love. Would you deny him this memory? Be patient, my dear; I know you do not mean your words."

"But I *do* mean them!" Catherine's voice held a cold note of anger I had not heard before. "I never liked Elizabeth."

"No, no," he protested, but she swept on with furious honesty.

"Oh *yes*," she said firmly. "There was always something almost *evil* about Elizabeth. I never knew what it was, but it was there." She paused briefly, then with a rush of words I heard her soft voice say "If it were to turn out that her spirit really haunts my brother—I should not be too surprised."

"Catherine, my dear!" Dr. Leon's voice was gently chiding. "I know. . "

I could bear no more. Stepping forward, I thrust open the door with one hand and looked at her angrily. "You should have learned by now,

Dona Medina, that it is wiser to close a door before conducting private conversations!"

"Wiser?" she echoed stupidly, and Dr. Leon whirled to her defense, "You eavesdrop in England, it seems?"

"In England, it is unnecessary, Doctor—but in Spain, and after the events of the last night, surely you will admit a difference between our countries?" I retorted coldly, and had the satisfaction of seeing his gaze fall from mine.

"From the first moment I entered this hellish place, I have been exposed to an endless series of lies, distortions, information withheld, and—hypocritical appeals for my sympathy."

Catherine's face flushed, then whitened to a deadly pallor that shamed me for my anger, but I was not minded to apologize. True and honest she might be, but already I had learned her knowledge was limited. Much had been hidden from Catherine, too, perhaps with the idea that her very innocence would be the more convincing.

As for young Dr. Charles Leon, I found his position among the Medina equivocal, a mixture of servility and altogether to great familiarity. However little I knew of Spain, I knew full well that the formality of its great families was rigid; where an English king might be friends with a simple squire, no such easiness existed on the continent. Then by what right did a mere country doctor—apparently little more that a superior midwife—address aristocrats by their given names? Was he, perhaps, a Medina born on the wrong side of the blanket? Nothing explained his intimate knowledge of the family and its foul heritage to my satisfaction.

And this was the man who had attended Elizabeth? So, far from convincing me all was well, I now suspected that *any*thing might have occurred . . . and Dr. Leon would contrive to cover it with his medical degree! How convenient for the Medinas—trained-to-the-leash doctor!

Turning, I stalked from the room amid dead silence. Then Catherine's voice said "Mr. Barnard!" I ignored her, continuing to the stairway; if breakfast existed, I meant to have some, and I did not think they would actually stoop to poisoning me, however inconvenient my presence.

"Mr. Barnard," she said again, urgently—and her appeal was suddenly crossed by a piercing shriek! Whirling about, I saw Catherine Medina standing frozen, one hand pressed to her mouth in terror. Behind her, Dr. Leon lunged into the corridor.

"What was that? Where did it come from?"

"Elizabeth's room," Catherine moaned.

Already I had regained the top of the stairs, and was thrusting past

Dr. Leon toward that suite "furnished with dedicated love," but before we could reach it the door swung open wildly and Maria rushed out, her face distorted by shock. She collided with the doctor's sturdy form in her frantic flight, and screamed again as his arms held her from falling.

"Maria!" Catherine came forward swiftly. "What *is* it?"

At sight of our familiar faces, she relaxed somewhat, but in the sobbing of her breath she still could scarce speak. Dr. Leon gave her a gentle shake. "What *is* it, child?"

Nerving myself, I stepped into Elizabeth's room, and found—nothing!

The room was silent, empty; in the center of the floor, mutely, lay a feather duster. That was all. What could have so terrified the maid? I saw nothing at all.

In the corridor, Dr. Leon had seated Maria on a bench, and was trying to calm her. "Easy, child," he soothed. "What happened to you?"

But she could only sob for man minutes, and it took all the doctor's most reassuring tones to produce any sense. At last, Maria sobbed, I . . . *heard her.*"

"Heard—?" We stared at her in horror.

She nodded her head, sobbing again. "*Yes,* I tell you I heard her, the *mistress!* I was cleaning and—and she spoke to me. She called me by my name, 'Maria.' She said 'Maria, *leave this room!*'"

Again she began to weep hysterically, while Catherine tried to comfort the girl. We had just got her slightly calmed, when she looked beyond us with a fresh scream, and the deep voice of Nicholas Medina said brokenly, *"No one shall ever enter this room again!"*

Dr. Leon arose from his seat beside the servant and tried to deflect Don Medina, but my brother-in-law stumbled hastily forward and with feverish haste pulled closed the door to Elizabeth's room. It was evident the sleeping potion still affected him, but his determination conquered the daze of his mind. "No one shall ever enter," he muttered, fumbling with the key and keeping one eye on me.

"No need to explain, Nicholas," Dr. Leon said quietly. "Mr. Barnard knows—everything."

Nicholas secured the lock and pulled himself erect abruptly, holding himself by his grip on the door handle and staring from Dr. Leon to me. Then finally, he shuffled past us toward his room, thrusting the key into the pocket of his dressing gown.

"See to the girl, will you, Catherine?" Dr. Leon said hurriedly, and hurried after my brother-in-law. Catherine looked after him anxiously, her arm still about the shuddering form of Maria.

I will see to her, Dona Medina, if you wish to go to your brother," I said coolly. I placed myself on the other side of Maria, drawing her from Catherine's arms to my own. Too distraught to consider any possible undercurrents to my offer, Catherine merely cast me a look of indecision, then abandoned the servant and hastened after Nicholas and Dr. Leon, closing the door of Nicholas' chamber behind her.

When we were alone, I gave Maria a healthy squeeze—she was not an ill-favored wench, for a Spaniard—and said briskly, "Now, I'll help you downstairs, Maria!"

"Oh, sir," she sighed, "The trembling in all of my limbs. . . ." But I had not dealt with servants all my life without learning a thing or two. In a trice I had drawn her to her feet, given her a hearty buss—*why* do the Spanish uniformly revere garlic?—and heading her toward the staircase, started her on her way with a firm smack on her buttocks. I was rewarded by a definite giggle!

"Now then," I said, tucking her arm in mine politely. "One step, then another step, and that's the way we'll go. . . ."

By the time we had reached the servants' quarters below I learned everything Maria knew. It wasn't much—but from the anxiety on Maximilian's face as he hurried forward to take her from me, I wondered what *he* thought she might have told?

CHAPTER THIRTEEN

AT LONG last we sat about the dining table, well furnished with eggs and bread, cheese and a variety of hot and cold meats. Dona Catherine toyed with her food, but Dr. Leon helped himself lavishly from the dishes Maximilian served. There seemed no diminution of his appetite due to the excitement of the last hours, and with this example before me, I felt capable of replenishing my own plate.

"Perhaps I should bring some food to Nicholas," Catherine said.

"He would not eat it, my dear . . . any more than you are eating yours," the doctor replied.

"I am . . . not very hungry."

"You need your strength, none the less," he said, and briskly slid the remainder of a fine cutlet from Maximilian's serving platter onto his own plate.

As the servant disappeared into the kitchen for a fresh supply, I grasped the opportunity to speak out. "If I may break into this most fascinating conversation with a question," I said bitingly, "how long, may I ask, do you intend to accept these *occurrences* at face value?"

Dr. Leon stiffened and turned on me sharply. "I should have thought, Mr. Barnard, that a man with your *investigative* zeal would already have solved the mystery?"

"And have *you?*"

"I am not certain, but you do remember that no one actually heard Elizabeth's voice? We have only Maria's word for it . . . ."

"I understood you to say that Don Medina has also claimed to have heard it." I retorted quickly, but he was not to be trapped.

"Exactly, Mr. Barnard," he said imperturbably. "'*Claimed'* to have heard it. I leave it to your own judgment as to whether or not he actually *did* hear it."

"And the harpsichord?"

He broke off a bit of bread, carefully sopped up the delicious meat gravy of the cutlet, and remarked casually, "You will find I believe, that Maria is more than capable of playing it."

"I see." As he transferred the dripping morsel to his mouth, I added, "And is she also more than capable of acquiring Elizabeth's ring . . *.from behind the brick wall of a tomb?"*

"Perhaps you have a *better* explanation," he said indistinctly.

"Perhaps I have. . . ."

He swallowed and looked at me sharply. "Well, then?"

"In questioning Maria before, I asked her to describe the voice which spoke to her."

"And?" he asked.

She could not describe it doctor—because it only *whispered to her!*"

Catherine and Dr. Leon stared at me, bewildered. "This point seems of vital import to you, does it? he commented. "

I was about to reply angrily, but was interrupted by a faint rumbling, followed by a crash. The noise seemed to come from above, and involuntarily we sprang to our feet, looking warily to the hall door.

Again we heard the noises, a perfect volley of bumps and thuds, that sent us running from the dining room and up the wide stairs to the bedroom corridor. There was here, no question of the source; Elizabeth's rooms—and behind that closed door, it seemed as if the interior were being demolished by a demon!

Shouldering Dr. Leon aside, I laid my hand to the door handle, but it was still as locked as we had left it yesterday. While Catherine and the doctor stared at the barrier, I whirled and ran for Nicholas' chamber . . . and behind me, the infernal din stopped abruptly. Instinctively, I halted briefly and turned to look backward, but the door remained closed.

Nicholas' door was closed, as well, and as I shortly discovered, it was locked! Furiously I pounded on the panel and shouted *"Don Medina!"* I rattled the handle fruitlessly, and repeated my shouts, but for a long moment there was no sound.

Then with a faint click, the lock slid back and the door opened—a mere crack—through which my brother-in-law's wan face peered at me in pitiable fright.

"The key to Elizabeth's room, sir!" I demanded, but he only stared at me in apparent non-comprehension. Impatiently I pushed at the door, and he stumbled backward, only saving himself from falling by his grip on the heavy wood. "The *key!*" I shouted, *"Give me the key!"*

With childlike obedience, he fumbled in the pocket of his dressing robe and handed me the key. "Again!" he muttered weakly, and made to follow me.

"No, do not go there, Nicholas! Catherine said fearfully, trying to restrain him, but he put her gently aside, saying "I must, my dear. . ."

I had not waited for his presence to unlock the door to my sister's chambers, and together with Dr. Leon, I burst into the room—to halt, aghast at the sight. "Good God!" he said, in a shocked undertone, while I stood speechless.

The room was a shambles, a total destruction! Silken gowns, dragged from the wardrobes, lay torn and crumpled upon the floor; mirrors hung, shattered and askew upon the walls, and the great curtains of the windows had been ripped from their fastenings. Beneath our feet, broken vases and urns littered and slashed the fine carpets with their sharp edges. The finely-inlaid tables sprawled among the debris; even the heavy carved chairs were overturned—and scattered amidst the wreckage were occasional eerie glints of precious jewels, their settings wrenched and twisted.

Slowly, the doctor and I stepped into the room, as Nicholas and Catherine approached. Don Medina's face paled and his lips trembled uncontrollably as he surveyed the scene. Then his eyes swung with a dreadful effort to the over-mantel.

With a deep groan, he took several stumbling paces forward and would have fallen had not Dr. Leon and Catherine rushed to support him.

The portrait of Elizabeth had been slashed to ribbons. Tattered strips of its canvas hung swaying in the chill draft created by the open door. I stood transfixed by horror; what demoniac hatred could have so deliberately destroyed the beauty of my sister's apartment? Who could have hated her so viciously—or could it, in very truth, have been the work of some ghostly visitor from hell? On the continent, I had heard, there were *poltergeists*, mischievous, tricksy spirits who delighted in making havoc in a home . . . but as Dr. Leon and Catherine led Nicholas away to his bedroom, I wondered. . . .

Alone with the wreckage, I picked my way carefully across to the wall and hesitated briefly, but the voices continued to retreat in the distance. Faintly, I could hear Dr. Leon urging Don Medina onward, "Gently, Nicholas, we are nearly there . . . one more step . . . and another. . . ." Finally, a door closed sharply, and silence surrounded me.

With feverish haste and all the careful determination I possessed, I began my task: feeling, pressing, turning methodically each protuberance in the panelling. I was obsessed by the conviction that, somewhere, I should find what I sought, for even at Chipham Manor, we possessed a secret passage (though it was most modest, being no more than a short flight of steps leading from the master's bedroom behind the great chimney and down into the servant's wing. Nor was it particularly secret, being known to everyone on the estate and merely used, in former times, by the bootboy to pick up and return my father's polished riding boots).

Nevertheless, a passage there *had* to be in Castle Medina; I was *sure* of it—else I must believe in a vengeful spectre. And though we know nothing of that world beyond death, I did not, would not, believe it was concerned in the events I had witnessed.

Moving step by step along the wall,stopping now and then to listen for any sudden return of the doctor or Catherine, I finally reached the fireplace. Later, I wondered why I had not started at this place . . . for exactly as in the master bedroom at Chipham Manor, I found the carved boss that turned and slid aside under my fingers!

On silent hinges, the hidden door moved back to reveal blackness, and with a grim satisfaction, I hunted among the broken bits and pieces of the room until I had found a usable wax taper. Lighting it from the flickering fire on the hearth, I approached the yawning shadows of the passage, and stepped through the entrance.

Larry Turner as Nicholas Medina, listening to his father, Sebastian Medina (Vincent Price), who is leading his faithless wife, Isabella (Mary Menzies) and his brother Bartolome Medina (Charles Victor) on a guided tour of his torture chamber, where the horrified young Nicholas will see his father torture and kill both his mother and his uncle.

CHAPTER FOURTEEN

IN THE feeble light of my candle, I saw before me a narrow stone passageway. My first thought was to secure my re-exit and, turning back, I spent no more than a minute in locating the inner sprint to the door. It was, in fact, placed exactly at shoulder height as in Chipham Manor, and in the midst of my adventures, I still was struck by that odd similarity. as though all secret passages must have been designed originally by the same hand. It seemed a useful discovery, and I put it away in my mind for later consideration.

Meanwhile, I had the satisfaction of opening and closing the door several times, making certain it would release me at my touch. In the light of my taper, I could see traces of fresh oil upon the hinges, and surmised frequent and recent use. But this was no more than I had suspected, and only increased my anger at the trickery about me.

At length, I allowed the door to swing closed behind me, and proceeded slowly along the passage. In the dark silence, my boots rang with unnatural loudness and I stopped often to listen for sounds of pursuit or surveillance. But nothing disturbed me as I made my way cautiously forward . . . to encounter *a blank stone wall.*

There was no question about it; the passage simply ended. Under the closest examination possible with my tiny flickering light, I could see no indication of a door, nor could my hand feel any handle, hinges, or lock; neither was there any inviting protuberance, concealing a spring. All was as smooth as if newly bee' waxed, though cold and repulsive to my touch.

I stood a moment in complete perplexity. Of what use was such a passage, leading only to an end dead as the grave? Again, I explored minutely but found nothing I had missed before, and finally I turned about, most unwillingly, and retraced my steps . . . to *success!*

A minute tinge of light indicated the door by which I had entered, but now I saw my error! Facing the other way, my taper dimly revealed the continuation of the passage on entering, I had turned right when I might with equal ease have turned left. With a quickening heart, I hastened forward, so sure of an eventual discovery that I no longer studied my path to identify and avoid some possible trap or pitfall that might hurl me to my death.

Then, again, I saw a minute tinge of light and ceased my steps abruptly, for surely another door lay ahead of me. Stealing pace by pace (and mentally cursing the clangorous nails of my stout English books which seemed to ring against the stone flags like a carillon), I crept near to the light and shaded my taper with an unsteady hand.

Dimly, voices came to me from beyond the hidden door . . . and in a second, I *knew* what I had only guessed before: here was Nicholas' bedchamber! Brokenly his sighs reached me: "What I have dreaded all these years has come to pass!"

"You are wrong, Nicholas," the voice of Dr. Leon responded, and from the faint clink of glass, I could envision him mixing a potion at the side table. "Now, drink this, my friend, and think no more on it."

"No, *no,*" Nicholas insisted desperately. "I tell you, she haunts me for the terrible thing which I have done to her."

I could bear no more; pressing the spring my fingers had already silently identified, I thrust back the door and stepped into the room. I found myself standing beside the fireplace, facing the great carved bed in which Nicholas lay against a mass of cushions.

The bedcurtains, heavy fringed and embroidered in an intricate pattern of gold thread, were pulled aside. Catherine and Dr. Leon stood anxiously, their backs to me, the one holding Nicholas' hand and the other proffering a wine glass from which my brother-in-law had averted his head in frenzied anguish. "Yes, Charles, she *haunts* me. . . ."

Twisting his head toward the doctor, he caught sight of me. I have no doubt my face plainly showed my contempt and disgust at this farce, for he shrank back against his cushions with a faint cry that caused the others to whirl about in fright.

"Mr. *Barnard!*" Catherine sighed, one hand pressed to her heart.

"What in the name of Heaven are you doing here, sir?" the doctor demanded angrily, and seizing the burnt feather from the night table, he bent to his patient once more.

Smiling coldly, I walked to the bed and looked down upon Don Medina. "And have *you* nothing to say?"

"What are you—" he muttered.

". . .*doing?*" I cut in swiftly. "Why—merely using the same route which *you* have been using, Don Medina."

"I don't understand you."

"Do you not? With your permission, I shall enlighten you."

"What is the meaning of this, sir?" Dr. Leon demanded.

"The meaning? Surely your own 'investigative' sense and *familiarity* between these walls . . ." I could not resist the reminder! " . . . Should tell you what I have discovered?"

By the spark in his eyes, I saw my shot had hit home. But he said only. "Have a care for my patient, if you please! And your 'meaning' is still obscure, sir."

"The meaning, doctor, is this: only *one* person in this castle could have caused all these inexplicable occurrences," I said. "That person is Don Medina!"

"What!" Catherine cried angrily.

"You are mad, sir!" Dr. Leon said firmly.

"*Am* I? I think not!"

Nicholas Medina opened his eyes and made a faint gesture of his hand. "Mr. Barnard, I *swear* to you—"

In my anger I was lost to all consideration for him, or those who now held and protected him. I faced the three of them and said in my strongest tones, "That secret passage sir—how convenient for you! Enabling you to whisper to Maria without being seen. Then, after the door to Elizabeth's room was locked—by *you* —enabling you to return and, at your leisure, to demolish everything!"

"You are wrong, sir, I *swear* I never—"

I swept over his protests. "You *lie!* When Maria screamed, *where were you?* Why were you not investigating long before the rest of us had come upstairs. When Elizabeth's room was being torn apart, *where were you?* Why were you no investigating the destruction of that room 'furnished with dedicated love'?"

"I . . . was afraid," he whispered.

"And I say that you *lie,* sir! Both times, you were in Elizabeth's room yourself! Both times your own door was locked, protecting you from discovery."

"*No!*" he cried. "God deliver me, no—it is not *true!*"

"I say it *is!*"

"And the harpsichord, sir? Dr. Leon cut in furiously. "Explain that, if you please—when you have already be told . . ."

"To paraphrase your own words, Dr. Leon—you will find, I believe, that Don Medina is 'more than capable' of playing it!"

Nicholas writhed against his cushions. "No," he insisted. "It isn't true! With sudden vigor, he threw off the restraining hands of Dr. Leon and Catherine and pulled himself from the bed, to stuble blindly toward the long windows. There, he caught himself by one hand against the curtains, his face distraught and his breath hard and rasping.

"Is it possible? he said in an undertone, and turned to us in terror. "Is it possible that I am doing all these things . . . *unaware* . . . to punish myself?"

"*For what?*" I broke in harshly, but Dr. Leon's voice overbore mine.

"No, Nicholas, *no!*" the doctor said firmly. "One of the servants is responsible. Most likely it is Maria.

Nicholas Medina ignored both of us. *"Could* I have kept the ring, without knowing it?" he murmured, dazed and fearful. "Could I have played the harpsichord, without knowing it? Or whispered to Maria? No," he told himself, *"impossible. . . ."*

Looking absently from the window at the mist rolling in across the battlements, he said, in a stronger tone, "Could I have used that passage . . . to destroy Elizabeth's room, all *without knowing it?* Is my inner mind creating evidence of Elizabeth's vengeful return because that mind *knows* that—"

He shook his head wildly and held his hand before his eyes.

"No," he said in a muffled voice, "I will not believe it. I adored her; even in madness, I would never have harmed her portrait, nor any least possession of hers." Straightening himself, with an effort, he said "But—how do I *know!* I do *not* know what I may have done. . . ."

Turning toward us, he loomed large and vigorous, as he said grimly, "I will find out." With a sudden return of vitality, he strode forward to the door, as we stood dazed and silent. It was Catherine who first grasped his meaning and cried, heartbreakingly, "No . . .no, *no!*"

"There is no other way," he told her. "I—must be *sure.*"

"For God's sake, *stop* him!" she pleaded, turning to Dr. Leon, but he only shook his head slowly.

"Perhaps it will be best, my dear," he said.

I felt completely at sea, as though the course of events had passed me by. It was only as I watched my brother-in-law withdrawing a heavy key from a drawer and turning to the door, that his intention reached me. Then, I, too turned to the doctor with a question in my eyes.

"If this is the only way of convincing Nicholas that he did not bury his wife alive, then I say, by all means do it," he said gravely. "This groundless dread must finally and forever be put to rest.

"But can he *bear* it? I asked with sudden anxiety. For observing Nicholas Medina measured steps to the door and into the corridor, I sensed the man was at the breaking point. Hastily Catherine ran after her brother, and I faced the doctor in the deserted room.

He was busying himself over his bag of herbs and simples. Withdrawing a phial with a sigh of relief, he tucked it in the pocket of his doublet and turned to the door, sparing me a glance of definite dislike.

"Your concern ill becomes you, sir," he snapped. "If I mistake not, it was your disbelief, your accusations, that brought Don Medina to this pass. You have left us no choice, sir—*We will exhume Elizabeth.*"

CHAPTER FIFTEEN

ONCE more we stood in the crypt of the Medinas. In out grim and silent journey to the bowels of the castle on the now-familiar route, Nicholas had led the way, uncaring who followed or if he travelled alone. Just so, might any aristocrat walk to the headsman's ax, or lift the poisoned cup to his lips, and I could not but admire my brother-in-law, despite my distrust of his motives.

With the strength of absolute determination, he had opened a small closet near the entrance to the crypt and chosen therefrom two heavy picks which he carried with perfect ease in one hand.

Unlocking the heavy door, he had tossed the picks within and moved deliberately about the walls, lighting every torch from the flambeau he had brought. Meanwhile, Dr. Leon removed his surcoat calmly, and hefting one of the picks, stood waiting. I could do no less, stripping off my coat, I pulled back my sleeves and possessed myself of the other pick, while Catherine pressed her clenched hands to her mouth.

Nicholas seemed quite unconscious of our preparations. When he finished lighting every torch, he moved toward that new masonry arch which fixed our attention and quietly took away the fine metal plaque with its inscription for ELIZABETH MEDINA. Then, turning, he sought for a pick, would have taken Dr. Leon's, who held it firm and shook his head in the negative. At the doctor's glance, I stepped forward, for it was my right to strike the first blow.

Bracing myself, I raised the pick and drove it full-force into the wall, chipping away the masonry that bound the bricks. Instantly, the doctor joined me, and for some moments our blows monotonously reverberated from the stone walls of the torchlit chamber.

Momentarily, Catherine gasped with shock and I whirled, pick upraised, but it was only her shuddering revulsion to a pack of rats disturbed by the noise, dashing across the floor in confusion. Nicholas stood as if turned to stone, observing our progress with detachment.

The work was far harder than I had expected. We had uncovered only a small portion when the doctor stopped and leaned panting against the wall. For myself, the sweat poured off me in rivers, but I would not give up. Slowly, carefully, I chipped away the covering from my sister's tomb, and when I had removed bricks to the extent that a man might have crawled through, Nicholas suddenly joined me, plucking the pick from an exhausted Dr. Leon.

He struck with an incredible force, as though driven and inspired by the toil. Working beside him, I redoubled my own efforts, and the echo of our blows nearly deafened me. Then, as one by one the bricks began to fall away from the tomb, I became aware that my brother-in-law was speaking, feverishly.

"Mother," he said, *"Mother!* Why was I not big enough—strong enough—to save you when father shut you away behind the bricks. . . I heard your pleading voice, I heard your scream, and I could do *nothing* as he set the last brick in place. . . ."

With every word, it seemed his strength increased, until, of a sudden, the wall crumbled and all the bricks fell in disorder, exposing Elizabeth's tomb.

It rested on a pedestal in the aperture, and in the flickering torchlight we stared at it in silence, feeling a superstitious dread at this disturbance of the dead. Then throwing aside his pick, Nicholas Medina pulled himself onto the internment shelf and strove to place his hands on the claps about the casket. For a space, his trembling fingers wrestled to unloose them.

Overcome by horror at the whole scene, I felt Catherine's hand clinging painfully to my arm, and instinctively set my own about her shoulder . . .but even without her delaying presence, I must admit I could not have forced myself forward to assist Nicholas.

Rapidly I glanced at Dr. Leon. His breathing now was even; he was completely restored from his exertions. Leaning on his pick casually, he was looking reflectively at my brother-in-law. And the thought came to me, "For tuppence you'd give him directions on how to raise a casket lid, you swine!"

Certainly, if anyone in our group knew the workings of such things, it must be the doctor! I felt sure a fair number of his patients must have ended within . . . and suddenly furious at the man's ghoulish relish, I put Catherine from me with gentle hands and sprang up into the shelf beside Nicholas.

Between us we loosened the last of the clasps; it slid aside with a grating noise, and straightening, our glances met across the casket. Don Medina was streaming with perspiration. He looked down undecidedly and hesitated; I sensed that even now, he might retreat. Reaching forward deliberately, I placed my hands upon my sister's casket—and instantly, he swept them aside.

Slowly he began to raise the lid. Glancing around I saw Catherine bury her face against Dr. Leon's arm, while the same inscrutable expression of half-enjoyment played over his face. There was no sound but Don Medina's gasping breath and the fitful spit of an occasional torch.

At the halfway point, he could bear the suspense no more. With a great heave, he tore the casket lid upward and back against the stone wall of the vault. Stepping back a pace, he faced me, panting, across the opening; our eyes met—and if I never see Hell, I shall still know its appearance from that demonic gaze.

With a cry, Catherine had lifted herself onto the internment shelf and clung to her brother's arm, while Dr. Leon stood beside me silently. Then, as if by some prearranged signal, we all bent forward. . . .

The sight that met our eyes was so terrible that even now it sickens me to recall it. Yet I must, if my tale is to be complete.

Within the handsomely embossed bronze casket lay blood and horror: three months dead, the partially decomposed, unrecognizable corpse faced us . . . contorted, mouth open in an eternal soundless scream of agony, with blood stains bespattering the inner side of the casket.

There could be no doubt: life had *not* been extinct for this corpse. Alone in darkness and confinement, she had tried fruitlessly to claw her way from her dread prison, leaving behind her the mute testimony of the life-blood smeared by torn fingers against the sealed and bolted barrier to air.

"I swear to you," Dr. Leon's voice broke and rose in a half-scream, *"I swear to you*—I thought she was dead. On my honor as a physician, I swear it . . . I would swear it on the Bible. . . ."

Catherine turned to me blindly, weeping soundlessly; I took her into my arms, lest she faint—but I looked at Don Medina.

He seemed on the verge of a total collapse, oblivious to everyone about him. Staring once more at the horrible sight before us, he backed away slowly, uttering a whimpering, half-mad sound that swelled up from his throat. "It was true," he choked, "all true—Oh, my dear God—it was *true. . . .*"

Turning, he scrambled away out of the vault as fast as legs could carry him and staggered through the door. His voice drifted back, *"Ture . . . true! . . .*

"*Nicholas!*" Catherine screamed, and pulled herself from my arm to follow her brother as rapidly as possible.

Left alone with Dr. Leon, we stared at each other silently across the casket with its dreadful revelation—and I had the satisfaction of forcing his eyes down. "I swear to you sir," he mumbled, "she was *dead. . . .*"

I turned away from him and descended from the shelf. Rolling down my shirt sleeves, I refastened their links and picked up my surcoat deliberately. Silently, he followed me. At last, I made my way to the door and stood, looking him up and down.

"Before *God* I swear it," he said.

"May I remind you of the First Commandment?" I replied. " 'Take not the name of the Lord Thy God in vain,'"

Picking up a flambeau from the wall, I went out into the subterranean corridor and made my way with all haste to the narrow staircase. I was crossing the great hall when I heard Catherine's anguished scream *"Nicholas, no! My God, no!"*

I took the main stairs two at a time, and burst through the half-opened door to Nicholas' chamber. Catherine held his arm in a steely grip, as he struggled to elevate a pistol to his temple. "Help me," she sobbed, "help *him!"*

Pulling her away from Nicholas, I struggled to unclench his fingers from the fire-arm. His strength was incredible, and for a moment I had given up; either he would shoot himself, or shoot me as I sought to get the thing away from him. Then of a sudden he capitulated. I took away the pistol and tossed it again into the open drawer from which he must have removed it, while he swung away from me, moaning "I *killed* her!"

"No, Nicholas!" Catherine told him pitifully. "Hush, it was not you, no!"

Sinking beside his bed, Nicholas Medina buried his face against the carved frame and repeated monotonously, *"I* killed her, *I* killed her—-it as *I*. . . ."

Catherine knelt beside him, cradling him in her arms, soothing, caressing, and he turned to her like a tired child. Together they sat, brother and sister, close-companioned in the age-old relationship of woman to man—her slender young arms holding his great trembling body, comforting and merciful.

Beyond the windows, the sky split in a slash of lightning; thunder deafened our ears, and the low boom of ocean surf against the battlements was lost in the roaring torrent of rain that deluged the castle. Involuntarily I sprang across to draw close the high windows, pull the long draperies into place. Thus it was that, standing in the farther embrasure, half-hidden by folds of velvet, I saw the entrance of Dr. Leon.

He stood motionless in the doorway; his body was perfectly controlled and at ease, and his expression, as he considered the Medinas huddled on the steps leading to the great bed, was blank—yet oddly satisfied.

CHAPTER SIXTEEN

BETWEEN the doctor and myself, we had raised Don Medina from his near-faint beside the bed and placed him in a great chair before the fire. Sternly, Dr. Leon had ordered Catherine to her bed.

"There is nothing you can do for your brother," he said, and when still she hesitated, he gently led her to the door and added, "Truly, my dear, you will only be in my way. . . ."

"But could I not just sit with him . . . out of sight, in a corner?"

"No," he told her firmly. "You, too, must rest, and to be certain of that, I will bring you a soothing draft in a few minutes."

She turned at once, her face alarmed. "Can you not prepare it now?" she said. "I promise to drink it . . . but Nicholas must not be left. I beg of you, do not leave him for even a moment!"

:Now, now," he said, patting her shoulder, "do not give way to these fears; Nicholas will be quite safe with me, I assure you."

Considering what had already occurred whenever Nicholas Medina was unattended for even a short while, I could not agree. Stepping forward, I said, "But I will be here, Dona Catherine. I swear to you, I will not leave this room until Dr. Leon has seen you to your chamber, delivered the sleeping draft, and returned."

Her eyes sprang to mine in deepest gratitude. "Thank you, sir," she whispered shakily.

But Dr. Leon interrupted fussily, "No, no, I cannot allow any disturbing presence in this room," he said. "You will leave also, if you please, Mr. Barnard."

"*When* you return, doctor," I told him pleasantly. "It is my right as well as my duty to remain near my brother-in-law, at this moment." He was half of a mind to argue, but I ignored him and turned to Catherine with a formal bow. "I give you my word *I will be here.* Go with an easy mine, Dona. Good night, and may you rest well."

She curtseyed to me with a faint return of color to her wan face, and went docilely from the room. After a moment's hesitation, in which Dr. Leon viewed me with no friendly glance, I had the satisfaction of observing his hurried preparation of the promised draft.

"Your presence is quite unnecessary, I assure you," he said in an angry undertone, as he mixed and stirred. "As Don Medina's medical attendant, I must protest, sir, and bid you to leave."

I turned from him indifferently, and busied myself in quietly adding logs to the fire. The storm still raged outside and the room grew chilly. Without looking, I said flatly, "I have given my word to Dona Catherine—and I have good and sufficient reason for keeping it." Shortly I heard him open the door once more, his footsteps retreating across the corridor in the direction of Catherine's chamber.

Alone with Nicholas Medina, I stirred the fire vigorously and added still another log. My brother-in-law, I saw, sat with closed eyes, but whether from exhausted sleep or to shut away the dread fancies of his mind, I knew not. My own mind held fancies equally terrible, though unquestionably different, and I wished for nothing so much as a time for deliberation.

I could not absolve myself of a vital part in causing the horror that had so affected Don Medina, and feeling that, were his eyes to open and light upon my face I should only revive his distress, I softly stole backward across the room. Carefully, I placed a small chair in the window embrasure, arranging the long velvet curtains both to conceal me and to cut off as much as possible of the dampness from the storm.

Then I sat down, peering from my hiding place every now and then to assure myself on my brother-in-law, but he sat ever before the fire without moving. Observing his handsome face in uneasy repose, a shamed anguish swept over me. Strange though he seemed, I thought we might yet have become friends under happier circumstances. I could have taken pleasure in riding the hills and woods of Chipham Manor, hawking with this man or hunting; introducing him to the beauty of England.

While of Court life there was little enough these days when Harry Tudor's sixth queen was more nurse than wife, still I could have been proud to present my beautiful sister and a noble Spanish brother-in-law. Like most Englishmen, I *feel* beauty rather than *understand* it, but from Don Medina I might have learned much that could have aided me with Chipham Manor. What, for instance would be his opinion concerning the carved music gallery I meant to add in the dining hall?

Now all was lost—and partly by my own hand. If only I had been content to stay at home, to let well enough alone and by a letter of inquiry, to ascertain—and accept—the simple fact of Elizabeth's death! Or, having come to Castle Medina, if I had only *believed* the harrowing tale my presence had forced Catherine to relate. . . .

But no! *I* had had to force my way among the Medinas, ruthlessly stripping away the decent privacy to which their family was entitled, purely for the sake of what I had conceived to be *my* family's honor!

Without my presence, Nicholas' sick delusions would have dimmed with time, and Catherine—sweet Catherine!—would have returned to her aunt in Barcelona or perhaps, accompanied her brother on a journey of forgetfulness . . .that travel he had planned with Elizabeth. And even though at the outset, that might have recalled its own sad memories to Nicholas, of those foreign lands he had meant to share with his adored wife, still, time inevitable heals.

Of course, had I stayed in England I should never have met Catherine Medina; she would long since have been betrothed to some suitable Spaniard of high degree. . . .

Putting aside this suddenly disturbing thought, I leaned forward to survey Don Medina. Still he sat motionless before the fire, but his position seemed more comfortable and I felt certain that at last he content to stay at home, to let well enough alone and by a letter of inquiry, to ascertain—and accept—the simple fact of Elizabeth's death! Or, having come to Castle Medina, if I had only *believed* the harrowing tale my presence had forced Catherine to relate. . . .

But no! *I* had had to force my way among the Medinas, ruthlessly stripping away the decent privacy to which their family was entitled, purely for the sake of what I had conceived to be *my* family's honor!

Without my presence, Nicholas' sick delusions would have dimmed with time, and Catherine—sweet Catherine!—would have returned to her aunt in Barcelona or perhaps, accompanied her brother on a journey of forgetfulness . . .that travel he had planned with Elizabeth. And even though at the outset, that might have recalled its own sad memories to Nicholas, of those foreign lands he had meant to share with his adored wife, still, time inevitable heals.

Of course, had I stayed in England I should never have met Catherine Medina; she would long since have been betrothed to some suitable Spaniard of high degree. . . .

Putting aside this suddenly disturbing thought, I leaned forward to survey Don Medina. Still he sat motionless before the fire, but his position seemed more comfortable and I felt certain that at last he'd be content to stay at home, to let well enough alone and by a letter of inquiry, to ascertain—and accept—the simple fact of Elizabeth's death! Or, having come to Castle Medina, if I had only *believed* the harrowing tale my presence had forced Catherine to relate. . . .

But no! *I* had had to force my way among the Medinas, ruthlessly stripping away the decent privacy to which their family was entitled, purely for the sake of what I had conceived to be *my* family's honor!

Without my presence, Nicholas' sick delusions would have dimmed with time, and Catherine—sweet Catherine!—would have returned to her aunt in Barcelona or perhaps, accompanied her brother on a journey of forgetfulness . . .that travel he had planned with Elizabeth. And even though at the outset, that might have recalled its own sad memories to Nicholas, of those foreign lands he had meant to share with his adored wife, still, time inevitable heals.

Of course, had I stayed in England I should never have met Catherine Medina; she would long since have been betrothed to some suitable Spaniard of high degree. . . .

Putting aside this suddenly disturbing thought, I leaned forward to survey Don Medina. Still he sat motionless before the fire, but his position seemed more comfortable and I felt certain that at last hetruly slept. With the greatest caution, I stole forth, placed more logs on the slackening blaze, and returned to my hidden post of observation . . . and my thoughts.

What now? There remained nothing, it seemed, but for a full apology from me and a rapid departure on the morrow. To remove myself from the castle might also remove, in some small measure, the memory of the harm I had done. Nothing could repair the ruined masonry in the burial chamber, nor the grisly spectacle it had revealed. Nothing would ever relieve Nicholas Medina from the horrifying knowledge that the very ghastliness he had feared was *true.* . . yet it could not be any fault of his.

The fault was Dr. Leon's!

All my original distaste for this vulgar upstart was now increased a thousand-fold by the memory of that tortured body in the casket—a memory I, too, could not bear to recall in any detail. The blood surged to my head and of a sudden I was suffused with heat. Involuntarily, I loosened the bolt of the long window behind me and gulped the cool air gratefully. The storm had passed, though scudding clouds across the moon warned me the relief was only temporary. We should have rain again before sunrise.

The normalcy of my country-bred observation brought me back to a semblance of sanity—yet if *I* had been so aroused, so overborne by emotion, how much greater must be the torture to Nicholas Medina in this circumstances? Casual and incompetent, *it was Dr. Leon alone who should now be lying exhausted in that chair before the fire, convicted by his ignorance for causing the death of his patron's wife!* Pressing my fevered head against the coolness of the window, my hand stole to the Toledo blade in my doublet; I longed to dispatch the doctor but knew this was not my right, but only that of Nicholas Medina . . . and in my brother-in-law's tormented mental state, I knew already that he would assume the blame for an underling's crime.

There was nothing to be done, and I was about to return to my post when I heard the click of the opening door latch. Some instinct for caution held me silent as I saw, between the long folds of velvet, the quiet entrance of Dr. Leon.

He stood motionless in the doorway, the empty potion goblet held in one hand—listening, observing, his glance ranging about the room carefully. At last, he seemed assured that I, after all, deserted my watch. He moved into the room with confidence, closing the door behind him, and murmuring, "He grew tired and has gone to bed, after all. . . ."

Setting down the goblet, he walked toward the fire, rubbing his hands together in a strange satisfaction. Nicholas did not stir, though Dr. Leon made no attempt at quiet in his demeanor. He looked at Don Medina for a long moment, then turned and tossed two logs clattering across the fire-dogs.

Still my brother-in-law did not move, and the doctor moved to the side table, poured a generous glass of wine and downed it at a gulp. With a pleasurable grunt, he refilled the glass and placing it on a second table close to his hand, alternately sipped and busied himself in repacking his doctor's bag.

Words cannot describe my fury and contempt for the fellow! Helping himself to fine wine while his patient slept! Walking about, humming to himself gently, with no thought for the man brought to this condition by *his* culpable hand.

I had nearly thrown aside the curtains, to step forth and rate him for the ignoramus he was, when he buckled his case and moved across to the wine service once more. Here he poured himself a careful glass (considerably smaller than his own, I noted) and carried it across to the fireplace.

"Nicholas?" he said. *"Nicholas?"*

Don Medina slowly opened dull eyes and stared at the doctor, who extended the wine. My brother-in-law gazed at the golden liquid for a moment, then averted his head once more. Dr. Leon looked at him appraisingly for a moment, then set the glass on the table at hand and seated himself in another chair.

"I would suggest, Nicholas, that you leave this place," he said. "Your remaining cannot help Elizabeth now."

Don Medina closed his eyes once more and drew a tortured breath, but the doctor leaned forward intently. "Nicholas, try to understand; I am a doctor of Medicine . . . if I could not deduce that she was—still alive—how can you possibly incriminate yourself for not being able to *know?*"

"Never in my career," Dr. Leon continued earnestly, "have I seen a condition which so completely paralleled the physical appearance of death. You cannot—you *must* not feel responsible!"

"All the time we were up here, mourning her," Nicholas said hollowly, "she was alive . . . struggling to be free of—" He hid his face in his hands with a groan. "I *am* responsible . . . it *must* be so; if it were not, she would not be haunting me."

"She does *not* haunt you, Nicholas," the doctor replied in the deep tones of assurance. "I beg of you—*believe* that you are blameless. . . ."

Ha! I thought, what a charletan the man is! What a pretty, persuasive scene!

". . . Can you not see now that these are all only hallucinations?" Dr. Leon laid a hand lightly on the fine brocade of Don Medina's dressing robe and said, meaningly, "Can you not see now that it has been you—yourself punishing yourself?" He paused with a sigh, withdrew his hand. "I must leave in the morning, Nicholas. Already I have been grossly negligent of my other patients. . . ." Again he paused, most effectively, and added "I beg of you leave with me!"

Slowly, Nicholas Medina turned, bit I thought his eyes did not see who spoke to him, nor had his minde absorbed even one word of Dr. Leon's specious plea.

"No," he said, and the casual, almost conversational, tone of his deep voice was like an accusing blow to my face in its sad acknowledgement of the dread fate *I* had brought upon him, "No, I can never leave. I must accept whatever vengeance Elizabeth chooses to inflict upon me."

CHAPTER SEVENTEEN

WITHIN my own bedchamber, I busied myself with the packing of my bags . . . avoiding the painted eyes of Sebastian Medina and his brother regarding me from the mantel wall. I had indeed been tempted to tear down both portraits and cast them into the fire. There was no doubt in my mind that Castle Medina would be the healthier for their destruction. But, of course, this was not my privilege and I stayed my hand.

As I gathered together my belongings and stowed them away, my thoughts were with Nicholas Medina—sitting bowed under intolerable guilt before his great fire. Following his refusal to quit the castle, he had sunk into impenetrable gloom, apparently impervious to all Dr. Leon's most earnest representations and medical commands that he quit the place at once.

I had stood in my observation post in a quandary: on the one hand, I wanted to be in my own room, preparing for my departure . . . yet to emerge from the window embrasure might only (since my brother-in-law's eyes were now open) remind him more forcibly of these events for which I felt myself so responsible. At last, I had gently pushed open the long window door and made my way across the battlements, trusting hopefully that in the general excitement, no servant might have thought to bolt my own window. And so it proved. My fingers found one glass panel free to their touch; in a twinkling, I had pulled it open and stepped, with relief, into the warmth of the Portrait Room.

My packing completed but for the last essentials, I considered my plan for the morrow: I would leave the castle—on foot, if need be—but leave it I would, and as early as possible after breakfast. Maximilian, I thought with a grin, would break his neck to aid me!

Perhaps there would be a farm cart, or some deliverer of provisions, for at this moment, I was by no means too proud or too nice to sit among chickens or cabbages!

I thought then of Catherine. I proposed to be gone soon after cock-crow . . . but I could not leave Castle Medina without a final word to her. It seemed vital to me that I tell her personally of my conclusions. After her bravery in revealing family secrets to me, and her loyalty to her brother, I owed *her* fullest explanation of my motives and resent emotions!

With no further consideration, I threw open the door to my room and approached that chamber I knew to be Catherine's, where I knock briskly—and had a sudden realization that once again I had blundered.

Full in the middle of the night, and at least an hour after she had retired and (to the best of my belief) drunk off a sleeping potion from the doctor, she should long since have been asleep; and now I proposed to rouse her? Appalled at my forgetfulness, I had nearly stolen away from her door when I heard her voice. "Who is it?"

"Francis Barnard," I said with a gulp.

I sensed she had approached and was just beyond the panelled wood, as she said "What do you want?"

"May I speak to you?"

There was a moment of silence. *She is recalling last night and her visit to my room,* I thought, *and wondering whether I have read too much into it!* At last there was a faint sound from the withdrawn bolt, and my heart leaped uncontrollably at this proof of her trust in me.

"Yes?"

"May I—come in?" I asked gently, "for only a moment. . . ."

She hesitated, then swung back the door—and walked away from me toward the window. Quickly I stepped over the threshold and closed the door behind me.

Catherine stood at the window, her arms clasped across her chest as if for warmth. Her luxuriant dark hair cascaded about her shoulders, lying as softly as feathers against the sea-green of her dressing Her face turned from me, she said again, "What is it, Mr. Barnard?"

"I have come to apologize to you," I said quietly, walking up beside her. She whirled and stared at me with an expression of fury.

"*Apologize!*" she said, contemptuously.

"Yes I know," I told her, quickly. "It seems that all my suspicions have been justified—but not as I had expected. I realize now that what happened to Elizabeth was an accident. I do not blame your brother. I feel only sympathy for him."

Her eyes scanned me fixedly and I added, "I assure you what I did was only for Elizabeth."

To my surprise, she said only, "You must have loved her very much."

"No, I scarcely knew her. She was raised in Europe, you know, and I in England."

Her pansy-brown eyes still held mine compellingly. "Then—why . . ."she asked.

"Why did I travel so far to investigate her death?" I said with sudden comprehension. "Because—oh, because I was not formally notified, because I remember Elizabeth as a madcap youngster, because I am the head of our family. . . ."

Before the sudden melting tenderness of her gaze, I looked at the floor.

"Because—I am a rude Englishman, if you will," I ended, "and thought. So, for the trouble I have brought to your family, I apologize, Dona Catherine.

Instantly her slim hand lay across mine. "Nay," she said, "there is no need of apology. We, too, were remiss. You had every right to suspicion us."

Her forgiveness seemed most angelic to me. I raised her hand to my lips, and found myself quite unable to release its softness. I fancied it warmed beneath my touch, and was not reluctant to be held.

"I am sorry that our meeting should have taken place under such unhappy circumstances," I said, at random. . . . I wanted only to be saying something, anything, so long as I might feel her hand in mine. "Had things been otherwise. . . ." Again I raised her hand to my lips and sensed the sweet perfume of her skin. "Perhaps we shall meet again in Barcelona, " I ended with a smile . . . and a fervent determination to spend my life in that town, if it would but give me a *sight* of Catherine!

"Perhaps in Barcelona, or," she smiled demurely, "in London?" As I stared at her in bewilderment, her mirth increased gently. "'Tis rumored my uncle—from Barcelona—will be ambassador to the new English court . . .Oh!" she caught herself in distress, "I should not have said that! You will not like to be reminded that your great king. . . ."

"Is dying?" I finished hardily. "But it is a fact, and an ending that must come to all men in time, Dona Catherine."

And in truth, I thought that at this moment I could accept the news of Harry Tudor's passing with complete calm. . . .

"I mean to be gone as early as may be tomorrow," I told her then, and felt mingled pleasure and sadness as her eyes widened in distress. "I shall ask Maximilian to aid me in the matter of conveyance; I expect he will be *delighted* to oblige," I added with a grin, and was rewarded by a sudden twinkle, quickly suppressed.

"So I will bid you good-bye, Dona Catherine," I said. Stepping back formally, I bowed. Automatically, she curtseyed . . . but as I turned and made my way from her chamber, she came up beside me swiftly.

"I bid you Godspeed, sir," she said breathlessly, "and pray for your safe journey." Holding the great door open for my passage, her dark eyes fixed upon me with a mixture of timidity and, I hoped, determination, "Until we meet again then . . . in Barcelona . . . or in London," she said, and swung to the door, leaving me, bemused, in the corridor.

CHAPTER EIGHTEEN

TURNING away from Catherine's door, I stood for a moment in the corridor, lit with its flickering flambeaux and silent in the depth of night. In the exhilaration of my parting from Dona Medina—and the hope I dared to entertain that she shared my sentiments!—sleep was far from my mind.

For a space I debated, and I will admit that my mind was far from clear or concentrated at this moment—but in between my recollections of Catherine's soft hand, and her adorable smile and *magnificent* understanding (for she seemed almost to know my sentiments before I could determine them myself!), I began to feel it rather right than enjoyable that I should also make a personal apology to my brother-in-law.

Uncertainly, I thought of my former diffidence to presenting myself before him, but I conceived that now I might tap on the door and consult with Dr. Leon. And despite that I felt him an incompetent butcher who should be slitting the throats of pigs for market instead of presuming to mix drafts and potions for denizens of a castle, I was in a mood to be polite, to accept his refusal to admit me to Nicholas' room, provided he would agree to present my message at a suitable moment.;

Accordingly I turned toward my brother-in-law's door. I had taken a few paces, when it suddenly opened, and Dr. Leon came into the corridor.

"What do you here, sir?" he demanded sharply.

Taken aback, I said, "I would like to see Don Medina."

"Why?"

"To apologize to him, I said quietly, supressing my start of anger at his tone.

Dr. Leon's face rearranged itself into a milder expression.
Stepping forward, he patted my arm and said "I wouldn't attempt to speak to him now. He has just fallen into a sleep, sir, after being—much overwrought. Perhaps in the morning it may be possible."

"I plan to leave in the morning."

The look of relief in his face was uncontrollable: just as I thought, he was the one person in the Castle who would be most glad of my absence! Without my visit, his bumbling incompetence might never have been discovered.

"Then perhaps you will accept the hospitality of my coach?" he said jovially.

I realized this was an opportunity not to be missed. Not only should I be conveyed away from Castle Medina, to which I had brought only sorrow, but alone with him in a coach, what might I not discover from this mountebank who called himself a doctor?

"Thank you, doctor," I said, with an attempt at equal joviality. "You are more than kind; I had been wondering whether I might be reduced to a seat in a farm cart among the potatoes.

He threw back his head and laughed heartily, and somewhat pallidly, I joined in his mirth. "But I would wish to take my leave of my brother-in-law," I said at last. "I would wish him to be assured that I hold him in no way responsible for my sister's death."

Dr. Leon's laughter stopped abruptly; once more he assumed the sober mien of the medical advisor. "No, I regret it is impossible. Oh, I know your fervent desire to make amends," he raised his hand in protest (though I had said nothing at all), "but as doctor to the Medinas, I fear I must forbid it.

"He is asleep; sleep brings peace and strength," he finished, and I could have shaken him for his pomposity! "He must not be awakened—instead, leave some message for him. Maximilian will provide writing materials, or indite the message for you, should you wish . . ."

I could only stare at the strutting jackanapes; did he think, I, Francis Barnard, an Englishman and head of our family, unable to *write?* I was hard put to restrain myself . . .but blissfully, it occurred to me that on the morrow, alone with him in his coach (and how came such a fellow to own a carriage at all? In England, our doctors jogged their rounds on horseback!), I should have ample opportunity to end this whole matter.

So I said only, "You are resourceful, doctor. I shall indeed leave a message if Maximilian will bring me the quill and ink-horn . . . and I must own, the sooner I am away from here the better. What time had you proposed to leave?

"As early as may be, following breakfast," he said.

Yes, I thought, you will never forego the chance of filling your belly at Don Medina's expense, will you?

"Then I will be ready," I said, and with the faintest of bows, turned away to my own room—when a thought struck me. Whirling back, I saw him heading to the main staircase and involuntarily I demanded, "And where do you go *now*, doctor?"

"Merely to the kitchen quarters—for fresh water," he said briskly, continuing on his way, then turning to reassure me, "Don Medina is full asleep, sir—pray do not be uneasy; I shall return in a matter of minutes. I bid you good night."

"Good night, doctor," I returned automatically . . . but as his steps retreated downwards, I could not restrain my sense of unease and distrust. I had promised Catherine I would remain with her brother earlier. Now, when the doctor had deserted his charge—although this scarcely surprised me—I was impelled to assume his duty.

I walked swiftly to Don Medina's door, laid my hand to the knob with perfect confidence—for had not Dr. Leon left the room but a minute before? The discovery that the door was barred and impassible shook me brutally awake! Had the doctor secured the door behind him as he left for his replenishment of water? I thought it impossible; surely, I had already been in the corridor as he stepped toward me and must have heard the sound of the lock if he had protected Nicholas in this way. . . .

Then—could my brother-in-law have awakened and bolted himself within as soon as Dr. Leon had departed? In Nicholas' disturbed mental state, I felt this entirely possible—but what dreadful event might not occur if he were not companioned and observed this night?

Quickly, I strode to my own bedchamber; I raced across the silent room to let myself out onto the battlements and make my way through the night shadows to the window by which I had left Don Medina's room some time earlier. To my relief, it was still open. Pulling it wide, I stepped through into the warmth of the enveloping velvet curtains. There I hesitated.

Let me reconnoiter, I thought; *if all is well, I will slip away so soon as the doctor returns. . . .*I was still uneasy at the possible effect a sight of my face might create with Don Medina. Drawing the curtains apart for an inch or so, I cautiously surveyed the room.

My brother-in-law no longer sat in his fireside chair! I had nearly parted the curtains and thrown myself into the room in a frantic search for him, when I saw his tall figure leaning wearily against the farther window. In his brocade gown, and with his dark hair and skin, he was half invisible in the shadow. He seemed reasonably at peace and content, staring out across the moonlit ocean, and I stayed where I was, content merely to observe and be at hand if wanted. . .

Slipping into the chair I had used previously, I was conscious of my weariness, but I meant to keep Don Medina within view until the doctor's return. It seemed a very long while that we rested—Nicholas at his window, and I in my chair—and the exhaustion of the last days had near overborne me with sleep, when I felt—rather than heard—a change.

Shaking the sleep from my eyes, I leaned between the curtains.

Nicholas still stood beside the farther window, but his figure was oddly rigid and he seemed to be listening to some sound I could not hear. "Yes?" he said, fearfully, "*Yes?*"

Then with a sudden effort, he found energy from some source within him. Straightening, he turned and surveyed the room slowly, while I shrank behind my curtain lest he spy me. Again, hidden in my darkness, I heard him say "Yes—yes, *my darling!*" and, "Where are you? Stay for me and I will be with you. . . ."

Frightened beyond endurance, I threw aside my curtains and stepped into the room, uncaring whether my face shocked Nicholas Medina or not. In the blaze of torchlight my eyes were uncertain at first. I saw my brother-in-law, his face alight with mingled hope and horror, but quite oblivious of me,turning,listening. . . .

In the stillness, I heard it clearly—a woman's voice, whispering urgently "*Nicholas . . . Nicholas . . .come to me, beloved. . . .*"

Before my terror-stricken eyes, Don Medina moved with incredible eagerness—and disappeared into the far side of the fireplace.

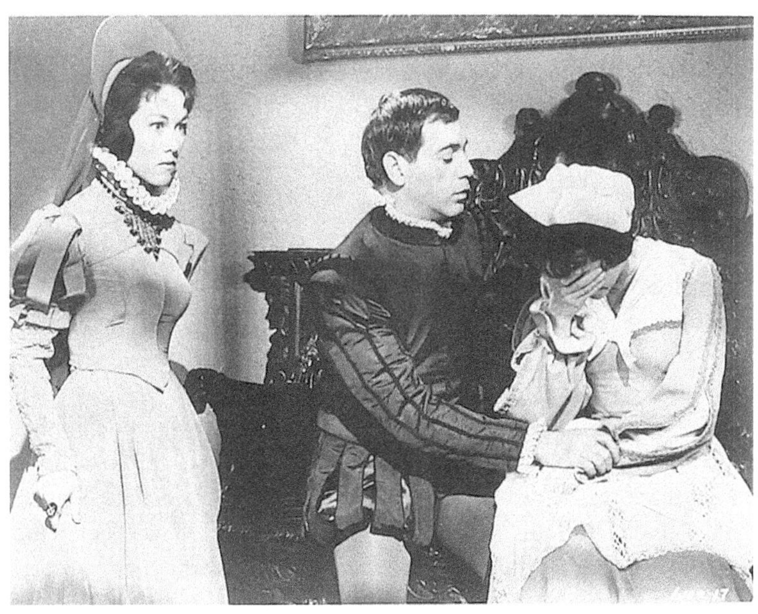

CHAPTER NINETEEN

"WAIT" I shouted, and raced for the hidden door . . .to find it closed in my face.

Frantically, I felt among the carved bosses but could not find the one I sought. As I twisted and pushed and turned them wildly, I tried also to consider what might be best to do. Should I unbolt the corridor and rouse the castle . . . or hope for Dr. Leon's return? The former course would only disturb Dona Catherine. And if my contemptuous estimate of the doctor were correct, he was happily engaged in sampling whatever wine was available in the dining room decanters.

Briefly I stopped my search for the spring to the hidden door to lay my ear against the panelling . . . and could distinctly hear faint footsteps and voices in the stone passage beyond.

Again the woman's voice enticed eerily, "*Nicholas!*" in a singing tone that made my blood turn cold. Even more distinct were the stumbling footsteps of Nicholas Medina; even more clear were the tones of his heartbroken voice replying "*Yes, yes my darling—Elizabeth, wait; I am coming, beloved!*"

My blood chilled as I continued my search for the opening spring. I felt convinced that just beyond my fingers lay a terror that might well send my brother-in-law to his death, and my only atonement for the tragedy I had unwittingly caused in Castle Medina would be my fine Toledo dagger . . .*whose hilt formed a cross.*

Setting my hand against it comfortingly in my doublet I had another idea—Elizabeth's room! If it were still unlocked, *there* I knew how to enter that secret passage! I sprang for the door to Nicholas' bedchamber, fumbling with the bolts . . . and in the corridor Catherine's alarmed voice shrilled *Nicholas!*"

"No," I called, "It is I, Francis—Nicholas is not here . . . one minute and I will be with you. . . ."

But I spoke to quickly. The door to Don Medina's bedchamber was not bolted, but *locked*—and I had not the key. Softly I spoke to Catherine through the door, controlling my voice as much as possible. The door is locked. I think Dr. Leon has the key," I said gently. "Do you wait in the passage, and I shall cross the battlements and join you through my own room!"

I heard her sobbing gently as I ran back across the room, thrust open the window and regained my own chamber. At last I had come up beside her in the hall, leaning against the door to her brother's room, her hands clenched fruitlessly about the handle and her breath faint and uneven.

With no apology whatever, I took her into my arms and held her gently for a moment, turning her back toward her chamber.

"Is my brother with you?"

"No," I said reluctantly, "nor in his room. But I will follow him so soon as I see you upon your bed again, Dona Catherine. Come now. . . ."

I had nearly persuaded her back to her chamber, when Dr. Leon came hurriedly up the great stairs. Despite the emergency, I noted that he carried no water container . . . but this was not the moment to inquire why he had abandoned his patient *in extremis. Let it pass,* I thought; he will have the more to answer for when I get him alone tomorrow!"

"What has happened?" he asked us in alarm.

"Nicholas is not in his room," Catherine sobbed. "I am afraid for him. After what happened this afternoon, why did *you* not stay with him as you promised me?"

"He insisted that I rest, my dear," the doctor said smoothly . . . *but that was not the excuse you gave to me,* I thought. Apparently flustered by this new development, Dr. Leon was badly caught off balance—yet in a twinkling he recovered himself and was turning to Catherine toward her room. "My dear, believe me, we will find him immediately!" Turning to me, he said, "Do you, sir, search this floor and the one above, while I look below."

Despite my resentment for his officious assumption of authority in delegating tasks to his betters . . . for I, and I alone, knew where Nicholas was to be found, and I had no wish for the doctor's company when I entered that secret passage once more.

Stepping backward with apparent humility, I watched him urging Catherine into her room, waited with impatience for his orders and civilities until he reappeared and looked at me with surprise. "I had thought you were gone upon your search, sir," he said blandly.

"No, I waited for to begin *yours*—so that our efforts might coincide," I returned with equal blandness. And as he turned briskly to the stairs, added, "Should we not arouse the menservants to aid us?"

"What?" he said sharply. "Heavens, no—by *no* means! What gave you such a thought?"

"Perhaps that another few pair of sturdy arms might be helpful," I said. "Who knows what we shall find this night?

"Nonsense!" he said testily, beginning his descent of the main stairs. "Don Medina would never forgive us if the servants were brought into this."

But even as he spoke, I was retreating swiftly toward Elizabeth's room, and he was out of sight as I laid my hand upon its door handle. Thank God, it was still open! Swiftly I stepped within, and picked my way across the wreckage, which still lay strewn across the floor, until I had reached the fireplace. It was illuminated only by intermittent moonlight; the clouds I had presaged a fore-runners of another storm were beginning to build again.

Twice I stumbled and might have fallen, as my foot struck an overturned table and slid in the folds of a silken gown, but at last I had reached the spot I had found earlier. Here, I was on accustomed ground; my fingers found the correct protuberance as if they had always known it, and in a second I had the hidden door open. Then I hesitated—for unlike my previous exploration, all was now blackness, nor was there any fire in Elizabeth's room from which to light a taper.

Undecided, I debated my course of action, while I found an overturned chair and kicked it into place against the open door, securing my return . . .Should I feel my way to the left, return to Nicholas' room (which I'd had no difficulty in entering from the passage this afternoon) and, propping open his end of the passage, possess myself of a taper for further exploration?

Was it even possible that I might, upon my return to Don Medina's bedchamber, find him already within . . . and no need for a search?

My indecision was settled by a distant sound of unsteady footsteps away to my right, and muted feminine voice, echoing dimly along the stone passage: "*Nicholas,*" it whispered. "*Nicholas . . . come to me, darling. . . .*"

With my hand upon the Toledo blade at my belt, I plunged blindly into the passage and stumbled to the right, unheeding of the clatter of my English boot-nails. . . .

CHAPTER TWENTY

A FAINTLY flickering light led me along that section of the passage I had first explored yesterday, and recalling its abrupt ending in an impassible stone wall, my heart leaped with grim satisfaction. Entering the passage as I had, from Elizabeth's room, I had cut off all escape or retreat for Don Medina, and that eerie voice he followed.

As I stumbled and slid along the stones, I could have shouted aloud in the excitement of the chase! *Now, at last I've got you—whoever you are!* I thought exultantly. *Ah, you forgot the secret passage had been discovered . . .and you never dreamed when you had locked Nicholas' bedroom door that I might have left an open window!*

I had reached the curve in the stone passageway, and deliberately I halted to catch my breath and pull together my defenses, before entering what I felt confident was the final scene. Mine was the hand that had created mush of this terror—and mine, I thought proudly, would be the hand to strip it open, lay it bare to the light of the day, and restore Don Medina to his own sanity.

Now that I, too, could hear this strange half-whispering voice, I felt angrily certain it was no messenger from beyond the grave. I have said I am not overly imaginative! Throughout my life and no matter how odd the circumstances, where *I* have heard voices, there have I also found only humans!

Then —who was my brother-in-law's will-o'-the-wisp companion?

With a deep breath I whirled around into the elbow-passage leading to the wall . . .but it was completely *empty!* With a cry of thwarted rage, I rushed forward . . . and brought up short to a sudden access of caution, *for where formerly I had found a blank wall, there was now a yawning entrance.*

The smooth stone wall was swung back upon itself, and from the flickering light which seemed now to be below me, I could only deduce a flight of steps. Still could I hear Don Medina's gasping breath and uncertain pace, and yet more clearly that voice floating gently, seductively, upward through the shadows.

"Nicholas, my love, follow me . . . come to me . . .I long for you, dearest . . . ."

And his answer, *"I come, I come—wait for me, Elizabeth. . . ."*

Now a chill of fear did strike me, and I hesitated. Certain as I was that the alluring creature who owned the voice was both human and viciously purposeful (though as yet, I knew not its aim), I was not minded innocently to be encompassed in that same unknown trap which might, I feared, await Don Medina. With feverish fingers I sought the secret of the stone wall . . .while the light below me diminished and slid away into silence. At length I had found the securing spring, though it was a slab of stone requiring all my strength to move its vital inch aside.

Then I once more grasped my dagger firmly and moved onto the top step of the staircase. The faint illumination by which I had moved was now deep below me. It seemed that the steps were narrowly entwined about a great stone pillar, probably one of the deep foundations of Castle Medina, and my heart pounded with angry frustration as I carefully felt my way.

One the one hand, I was tempted to shout a warning to my brother-in-law—yet I knew that were my alien voice to resound through the passage, all hope of catching my prey and identifying the source of these disturbances must end.

If I were to settle the mystery, once and forever, I must give no hint of my pursuit; somehow, I must contrive to step forth at the precise moment when the unknown disaster appointed for Nicholas Media could simultaneously be revealed and balked.

Accordingly, I made what haste I could, but it was only my angry determination that prevented an instant return to the open rooms beyond the upper passage. For surely no more loathsome experience has ever come my way. My fingers caught against the rough-hewn stone that walled the stairway, and felt a nauseous slime; squeaks and scuttering indicated this foul pit was fully populated with rats.

Indeed, so unaccustomed were they to disturbance by humans that they tumbled across my boots and one sprang upon me viciously, fastening its fangs so deep into the leather as to be carried several paces before I kicked it free with a shudder.

Tattered cobwebs still festooned parts of the walls, where they had been flung by Don Medina's earlier transit but twice I brushed an immense furred spider from my face, as it wildly sought to repair its web. Unlike the secret corridor linking Elizabeth's and Nicholas's rooms, this passage I realized had been little used for long years. Where was it leading us . . . and who was our guide?

Might it, after all, be Maria, as Dr. Leon had suggested? Bur for what reason would a servant so harass and frighten her master? Nothing I had seen in my encounter with Maria yesterday bespoke her as mad! I should, in fact, have thought her most definitely the simple ignorant peasant girl she seemed . . .and exactly the one to be most vulnerable to superstitious occurrences. Aside from Nicholas Medina himself, she was the perfect choice for immediate and absolute belief in some spectral visitor.

Maximilian? I hesitated, mentally. The voice, luring me downward *could* be that of a man, disguised in a falsetto whisper—but in only two paces, I felt positive it was not the servant. Despite his original reluctance to admit me to Castle Medina and his taciturn expression, I had sensed a devotion in the man for both Dona Catherine and Nicholas Medina.

Dona Catherine had stoutly maintained the absolute loyalty of the servants to her brother and while her tender woman's judgement might be tricked, I was inclined to believe her correct in this instance, I had felt a deep integrity in Maximilian, a gradual relaxing of his defensive suspicions—and when I had come upon him suddenly as he supervised the freshening of my chamber earlier this day, I had thought him half of a mind to converse with me.

No, it was no more Maximilian than—than Dona Catherine herself! There remained only Dr. Leon . . . and my conclusion, I realized, caused me no surprise at all! Nevertheless, it lent speed to my steps and promptly brought me to grief, for I slipped on the damp stones and slid painfully against the retaining wall.

Scrambling erect, I discovered I had wrenched my ankle. But more importantly, I was within sight of my quarry—for just ahead, around the final curving steps, I saw a second great stone slab standing open.

As my eyes absorbed what lay within their vision, I recognized the dim plaques and mourning candelabras, and knew that I should long since have guessed where our steps tended.

The stairs had led us to the burial crypt of the Medinas.

Within, the light increased slowly and I surmised the tall form of my brother-in-law, hastily kindling the wall torches from the flambeau he held. As he moved about, he spoke, *to Elizabeth,* with pet names and endearments that both anguished my heart and brought a chill to my blood . . . for in that lighted crypt, with its blank bricked walls, what had become of the lure that had brought him?

Now I could see him; in his voluminous brocaded robe . . .lighting a final torch and turning with an expression of wild terror, to stare at a point beyond my view . . . I knew what it was, however: the shattered tomb of Elizabeth Medina. That internment shelf with its pedestaled casket and broken masonry must, I knew, lie directly to my left on a line with the opened door. The main door to the crypt leading into the subterranean corridor down which we had come twice in the past hours was clearly visible ahead and slightly to my right.

Then—again—the faint whispering voice *"Nicholas . . .dear Nicholas!"*

It sounded so close at hand that for a half second I almost *believed* in a ghost . . . for where was a hiding place in that outer chamber, yet from Don Medina's eagerly searching eyes I knew *he* saw nothing!

"*Yes,*" he said and hastened forward, his awkward shambling gait taking him out of my view. From the sounds, however, I realized he had once more painfully drawn himself up onto the shelf beside Elizabeth's casket. Within the stairway, I stole forward as quietly as possible, cursing the twinge in my ankle, and stooped low to peer cautiously around the stone door.

It was in my mind that I might yet remain undetected a while if my head emerged below the angle of vision from that tomb . . . and that in spite of my aching ankle, I might still have the advantage in any melee through springing from a kneeling position at a decisive moment. But never had I expected what I saw.

Nicholas Medina had crawled into the tomb beside my sister's casket. Fearfully, timorously, uttering small whimpering sounds, he moved one step at a time, always approaching that dread symbol of finality and death. Twice he stretched out his trembling hand to the lid, and twice withdrew it quickly; twice he half-turned to flee, and forced himself to turn back.

Yet—*I saw nothing.*

In spite of myself, I trembled with the beginning of a fear to equal my brother-in-law's. Convinced of a human source to this tragedy, I had relied on my arm, my dagger, and the advantage of a surprise attack. But what if, after all, *this were no human mischief?* How, then, would I protect either myself or Don Medina?

My dependence, then, must be all upon the efficacy of that small crossed dagger hilt, but I knew not if it could suffice to save us both.

Before my starting eyes, the casket lid stirred slightly, *raised* itself an inch—another inch! With a deep groan, Nicholas Medina shrank back against the inner wall of the tomb, while the casket lid continued slowly to rise. Helpless, transfixed, he stared at the inexorable lifting . . .*lifting!*

Nor will I deny my own horror at that moment! I could only, with an inborn instinct for preservation, reverse the digger in my hand to hold it, half upward, pressed to my breast.

Then with a final motion, the casket lid was fully raised and crashed back against the rear wall of stone. Instinctively my eyes closed in a wince against that echoing noise; when I looked once more—*a bony hand had appeared at the edge of the coffin!*

Sinuous as a snake it felt its way over the edge, grasped it firmly, and slowly, from within, a figure emerged. It pulled itself upward, stiffly and jerkily; its head was swathed in a cere cloth from which the vile stench of mold permeated the crypt.

"*No,*" Nicholas whispered, and my own involuntary cry was lost in his greater scream: "*No!*"

Frantically, he turned and half-tumbled from the shelf. The torch in his hand swung so wildly that it nearly fired the full silken folds of his robe. Tripping on the hem and sobbing madly, he staggered past me toward the outer door of the crypt. After a moment's fumbling, he threw it wide and disappeared into the outer corridor.

Within the casket, now the figure uttered a wild, shrill laugh, pulled itself more swiftly up and over the edge of the box to stand upon the floor of the crypt. "*Nicholas!*" it murmured, moving toward the corridor door. "*Nicholas, my darling . . . come to me . . . wait for me. . . .*"

Half-fainting at the grisly sight, I knelt behind the stone door, and the apparition swept past me, oblivious of my presence, to pause a moment at the door. Impatiently loosening the hampering folds of the grave clothes with a kick of its foot. it uttered a second ringing peal of laughter and ran into the passage, following Nicholas Medina. Floating back to me, echoed that seductive voice—but now it held a note of derision.

"*Nicholas—why do you run from me, dearest? Nicholas . . .wait!*"

For a long moment, I knelt, stupefied by the scene I had witnessed. Within the burial chamber, all was silence broken only by the fitful torches. Slowly I arose—and found myself still holding the Toledo dagger upright before me. Trailing across the threshold of the corridor door lay a length of the foul-smelling winding cloth . . . and in another moment my mind had cleared, to convince me of my sanity in the face of every occurrence.

That—*thing*—which had pulled itself from the grave to pursue Don Medina was, I knew, entirely flesh and blood, though unquestionably more mad than the man it pursued.

For the dagger belt I had unconsciously raised against its presence, I now saw was fashioned in the representation of Our Lord Himself . . . and had the apparition been from another world beyond the grave, it would infallibly have been thwarted and forced to disappear.

Instead, it had passed me, to lean against the lintel and laugh, before continuing on its way. In an instant I had emerged from the secret door, traversed the crypt and, stopping only to seize a torch from the nearest wall holder, had turned into the main corridor behind it.

CHAPTER TWENTY-ONE

FAR ahead of me down the corridor, I could hear the stumbling footbeats of Nicholas Medina, and in the lighted patches (for only an occasional flambeau had been left as a night light) I could see his figure staggering drunkenly from one side to the other. Behind him glided the dread figure in its remaining grave clothes. Convinced as I was of its human composition, the lack of any footsteps disturbed me not. No doubt the Creature had prepared its shoes with deadening cloth about its feet.

My progress was maddeningly slow, due to the wrenched ankle which throbbed villainously—and still I dared not yell, for at all costs I was now determined to unmask the spectre. Hobbling as quickly as I could, I dimly glimpsed Nicholas Medina disappearing into the corridor leading to the torture chamber—and in another second the pursuer had vanished after him.

Yet what I could not see, I might deduce from the sounds that echoed back to me: a tinkle of metal betokened the key to the chamber; the choking gasps and the scrabbling noises told me Don Medina had dropped the key in his haste and was wildly seeking it on the stone floor. . . . There came another peal of laughter, interspersed with the whispered "*Nicholas, Nicholas, my darling . . .*" but now the tone was frankly derisive.

For the first time I regretted that I had not insisted on rousing Maximilian and two or three stout footmen before undertaking a share in this chase. Sturdy as I was, I feared I might not be capable of bringing the thing to an end alone and unaided.

It seemed impossible, too, that no one should hear the terrible sounds echoing about my own ears, but perhaps it was too much to hope that servants would rise from their pallets to investigate. Nor could I blame them for hugging their beds and pulling the coverlets about their ears against the gasping sobs and mad laughter. At this moment it was only my own certainty of a foul, but completely human, plot that drew me forward along the corridor only half-lit by an occasional torch with full night-shadows between.

I had reached the protecting darkness of one of these spaces when there was a tremendous crash of sound. I thought Nicholas had finally managed to open the door to the torture chamber and violently slammed it behind him, and with a sense of relief I hesitated to draw a breath. The dead silence which now surrounded me was more shocking than the former clamor, but my eyes could not discern any return to the main corridor of that gliding figure.

Making my way forward again, I had nearly reached the side corridor when I heard footsteps about on the stairway leading to the great hall. Swiftly I retreated into the closest patch of darkness and waited, rubbing the blood back into my ankle as I stood. It seemed, then, that everything happened at once.

I had no more than regained the safety of shadows than an approaching footsteps became those of Dr. Leon, calling urgently, "*Nicholas! Nicholas, where are you?* Answer me."

Under one of the farther torches, I could see his face was gaunt with worry, and I had nearly stepped forward to seek his help for an attack on that *Thing* beyond us, when once more there was the crash of the torture chamber door.

It was followed by a heart-rending shriek that could only be Nicholas, and a wild feminine scream: "*Nicholas!*"

The doctor paused briefly, then an unmistakable smile crossed his face! He broke into a run and vanished into the corridor.

Then did I put on all speed, ignoring the pain in my ankle—for with the sight of Dr. Leon, much of my solution had fallen apart. The scream had been completely identifiable as feminine; it could *not* be Catherine, and I felt sure it was not Maria.

Who, then, was in the torture chamber with Nicholas? As I, too, turned into the corridor, Dr. Leon stepped through the door and thrust it closed behind him—but not before I had heard that most dreadful of all sounds: the laughter of the insane.

It started as a chuckle, rose to a full laugh, and ended in a shrill demented cackling , , , and as if I had already entered that chamber, I knew it could only be Nicholas Medina. Limping rapidly to the door I turned its handle expectantly for I had heard neither bolt nor key as the doctor entered. But the door swung back only a scant six inches, and I saw that it was held by a stout leather thong, looped over a nail placed beyond my reach.

All the while that soft insane laughter filled my ears . . . but now I could see at least partially into the chamber. Before me stretched the stairs, partly obscured as they twisted downward, but again revealed where they debouched onto the stone floor. Lying on the floor, half propped against the wall—as if he had fallen down the stairs and rolled into his position like a rag doll—was Nicholas Medina. Soiled and bedraggled, his brocade dressing gown was twisted about him. His face was smudged from the foul cobwebs of the passage we had traversed.

His hair disarranged, his head lolling idiotically, a witless smile for his expression. I caught my breath in horror. There was no doubt: Don

Nicholas Medina was totally, hopelessly out of his mind through the occurrences of this night.

Dr. Leon stood, back toward me, at the top of the stairs; at his feet the remainder of the filthy cere clothes dribbled across the balcony floor onto the top steps, as if cast aside in rapid passage. Even through my narrow peephole, I thought I could smell, faintly, their disgusting odor of rotting death.

I had nearly called to him softly, to apprise him of my presence and aid in recovering Don Medina . . .when I saw the figure kneeling before my brother-in-law. It was a woman, clad in a white satin gown besmeared with slime. She threw back her head and laughed . . . and as if matching her laughter, Nicholas chuckled and giggled, pointed his finger at her and twisting into further chuckles and giggles, as he rolled from side to side against the stone wall.

Together they sat, in a paroxysm of hideous mirth—and on a sudden the darkness was split by a vivid flash of lightning. The storm had returned, but as if it marked a turning point, Dr. Leon hurried down the stairs.

"I told you to wait!" he said angrily.

The woman looked at him over her shoulder for a second. Then she rose with a lithe movement, tossing aside the cloud of night-black hair that had slipped from its pins, and said fiercely, "I couldn't!"

In the vivid flash of lightning that illumined the torture chamber, I recognized—*my sister Elizabeth!*

I think my heart skipped a beat, but there was no question that it was she—quite fully alive in all her delectable flesh. Hers was a beauty no besmirched gown, dirty hands, nor disarrangement of tresses could dim.

Further, as I stared at her now, I realized that I, no more than Nicholas, had really been able to believe in the extinction of so much vigor and voluptuous greed for living. Impossible to believe in an Elizabeth dead by any other means than some shocking violent cataclysm—a fall while hunting, or drowned on a picnic, inadvertently pierced by an arrow or buried beneath and avalanche. *These* were the sorts of things that would happen to such a vital spirit, and never anything so—so *timid* as expiring of fright in her husband's arms!

Then . . .*why*, and *how*, and for what *reason* had she made this pretense of death? Looking at the placidly gibbering face of her husband on the floor behind her, I knew with a sickened heart that all was intentional . . . for I suddenly *remembered* Elizabeth!

The first child in the family, for a long while the only daughter, and with something of quickness beyond the average in female children, Elizabeth had been the particular pet of my father. He had delighted to set her on a blood-mare when she was scarce able to toddle—and had tossed her to the skies for her ability to clench the reins and control the beast.

Often had my mother told me of the two sons she had lost between Elizabeth and myself, and shaken her head sadly, saying "'It would have been better for Elizabeth had one of them lived." Too sadly true, I thought, for father had spoiled her badly, or on our mother's death, our aunt had spoiled her even worse with her emphasis on beauty and jewels and wealth . . .

Now she stood, bedraggled yet incredibly, breathtakingly beautiful, surrounded by the foul instruments of the torture chamber and, as the storm increased in strength, her face stood out in each flash of lightning.

But I liked not its expression of *brutal* triumph!

Pushing her aside none too gently, Dr. Leon knelt in her place before Nicholas Medina, moving his hand professionally backwards and forwards before my brother-in-law's eyes . . . but there was no reaction whatever. Nicholas simply stared into space and ever and ever and again chuckled uncontrollably, as through suddenly reminded of some hilarious private joke.

At last the doctor rocked back on his haunches and said casually, "Well, my old friend, it seems a happy world you've entered!" Then he stood and turned to Elizabeth with a smile. "He is gone," he told her. "totally gone."

"Good!" she said, and even the doctor recoiled slightly at her tone of satisfaction. For a moment she stood, looking down at Don Medina . . . then she turned, and with a passionate movement flung herself against the doctor.

"Charles," she murmured. "Charles, my beloved."

Before my sickened eyes, I thought he held aloof for a moment. Then as if unable to resist so much luscious beauty, his arms went about her and their lips met in a lingering kiss. Still holding her he muttered, "All right, it's over—all over . . . ."

Now the whole vile story was clear enough to me; I was perfectly cold and objective. No matter that Elizabeth was my sister; she was a disgrace to her name. Not did I any longer feel responsibility for the tragedies of Castle Medina in the past two days; I might perhaps have hastened them, but even had I never come to Spain at all, the vicious in explicable plan conceived (I was certain) by my sister would have run its course.

Coldly I assessed the figure of Elizabeth pressed against Dr. Leon, exchanging kisses of savage passion, and coldly debated my course of action. Could I retreat quietly, get myself up the stairs to the servants' quarters, rouse Maximilian and a few stalwart aids, and return before Elizabeth and her paramour might have dispatched Don Medina forever?

Judging by their embraces and murmured tenderness, the guilty pair felt entirely secure at this moment. Completely unaware of my observation, and brutally disinterested in the witless presence of Elizabeth's husband, they lingered and kissed and caressed with abandon, while Nicholas Medina rolled his head back and forth against the stone wall and occasionally laughed wildly.

I had decided to chance it and race away for aid, when Elizabeth drew herself from Dr. Leon's arms with decision. "What about my brother? she asked . . . and I learned to open the door with renewed interest.

Yes, I thought, *what about your brother—what have you planned for him, you trollop!*

The doctor was by no means through with his embrace, but when he would have pulled her again to his arms, she held herself aloof, and repeated, "What's to be done with Francis?"

"Oh, he's to leave in the morning," Dr. Leon shrugged, and added with a dry chuckle, "he's accepted a seat in my coach!"

Elizabeth pulled herself entirely away from his arms and took a swift turn about the floor, ignoring Nicholas who was singing softly to himself and making a cat's cradle in the air. "I like it not," she said. "Francis was ever a nosy brat, who observed everything and looked as though butter would not melt in his mouth . . . until he opened that mouth at the most awkward moment!"

"Truly, he does have a most inconvenient way of pouncing on the very point one could wish him to miss," the doctor said thoughtfully. "Still—he's seen little, talked to no one but Catherine. I think he's calmed; only a short while ago, he was of a mind to apologize to Don Medina for all the trouble he'd caused.

She spared him a sardonic smile for this, but looked grave again. "All the same," she said, "I conceive him a danger Charles. 'Twould be better if he never returned to England . . . ."

"Perhaps," he said uneasily, and she whirled to press herself against him again.

"See to it," she said, muffled.

But she had overshot her mark, I saw. Now it was he who stepped back, troubled by her command. But whether because of it tenor or because he was unsure how to carry it out . . . I was not certain. "He will leave in the morning," he told her evasively, "but—*why* could you not wait one more day?"

"I have waited long enough," she returned, and kissed him again.

The violent sensuality of her caress no longer disturbed me, I found.

Yes my darling sister, I thought, coldly dispassionate, *you were ever a reckless bitch who would not wait a minute to enter Heaven—but now it will be your undoing. If only you had waited until the morrow when I was set for England, all would have gone to suit you.*

And of course, it would have—for once removed from the castle I should have received the news of Don Medina's complete mental collapse as sad, but understandable. I should have raised no questions, nor returned again into Spain—particularly if Catherine were (as she hinted she would), to come to England.

But Elizabeth was never patient, and now—it would cause her downfall. My sister or not, I would see her taken and hanged, if need be, for her treatment of Don Medina.

Nevertheless, without other witnesses, I was in a most awkward spot: an Englishman, in Spain, with God knows what concocted tale between Elizabeth and the doctor. . . . It seemed I was like to perish any way I turned—either in the coach by the hand of my sister's lover, or by the King's Tribunal.

While I hesitated, and yet cursed myself for not running to summon Maximilian, Elizabeth tore herself once more from the doctor's arms and knelt with a vicious triumph before the broken figure of Nicholas Medina.

"So," she crowed—and that did *sicken* me, for how well I remembered that pleased note in Elizabeth's voice as a child when she had, at all costs, gotten her own way! "So, my dear darling husband . . . we have broken you at last!"

Even Dr. Leon was uneasy at her tone. "Elizabeth—my dear, there is no time for this. . . ."

"Oh yes, there is time," she told him bitingly. "I have waited long for this moment. . . . Yes, there is time for me to bloat. . . ." She laughed—and Nicholas laughed with her, holding out his hands to her like a baby. She trailed her fingers across them like a mother playing with her child, then gave them a petulant slap from which Nicholas recoiled with a slight whimper of dismay.

"*Now* you are as I want you," she said. "Gibbering and helpless . . . and according to your last will and testament, your 'dearest oldest friend, Charles Leon' becomes the guardian of your estate. And you own so much, don't you my darling? So much gold and silver, and lovely castles, and fine fat herds of cattle . . . to day nothing of the lovely, lovely rubies and diamonds and pearls you've given me!"

With a swift motion she unfastened the glistening string of jewels from her neck and holding them in one hand, turned and twisted them before

Nicholas. He laughed gently, happily, stretching a hand, like a child, to clutch at the bauble, and pouting when she withdrew it tantalizingly just beyond his grasp.

"*Wealth!*" she said. Jewels and carpets and fine food and having my portrait painted in Madrid. . . . Why did *I* have to live in this damp country house? You said you loved me, why was I not a part of the courts—Paris, London, Madrid?

"Nut now . . . I shall have it *all*, Nicholas! All! My poor stupid husband, with your 'dedicated love' and 'no hand but mine.'" Her voice rang with a lilting laughter.

Dr. Leon shifted uneasily, and laid a restraining hand upon her shoulder. Enough, Elizabeth," he said, but she only shook him from her.

"Did you *enjoy* the sight of the woman we put in my coffin, Nicholas?" she asked, lowering her voice to a ghoulish glee. "Poor thing! Charles found her wandering along the road, with no home, no money, no relatives, no future . . . so he just gave her a little something to drink."

"No," Dr. Leon protested, but she merely smiled at him.

"Is it my fault you didn't make the dose strong enough?" she asked him sweetly, and returned to her sport with Nicholas.

"You never knew about the secret passages, did you, *dear Nicholas,*" she cooed. "I found you father's drawings for them . . . it was almost *too* easy !" She laughed softly, as Dr. Leon caught her shoulder with a firm grasp and said angrily, "You are a *fool,* Elizabeth! Give over, give over—there will be plenty of time for this. . . ."

She threw aside his hand with blazing glance and said "I tell you there *is* time for this. . . ."

"And *I* tell *you,* your brother together with Dona Catherine and half the servants will be here any moment! he told her with unsuspected firmness. "Come away now, and let us complete the plan. . . ."

"When I am *ready,*" she said arrogantly, and leaned closer to Nicholas's dazed happy face. "Is it not ironical, my husband," she said seductively, "Your mother was an adulteress—and your wife—your uncle an adulterer . . . and your closest friend an adulterer. . . ." She laughed softly. "Don't you find that amusing, *dear* Nicholas? . . . If you come to think of it, practically everyone of their close friends and relatives!"

Again, she laughed and Nicholas Medina stared at her mutely, uncomprehending, for a moment. A variety of expressions passed over his deranged features, as if he would join her laughter—then grew afraid—and half-laughed again, snatching at her gleaming string of jewels. Childishly, he sought to repeat her words.

"Adulterer," he mimicked, thickly.

"Yes," she returned mockingly. "*Now* you know!"

A moment passed in which he sat silent, head lolling, his eyes fixed upon her dully. Then he smiled, and began to laugh quietly . . . menacingly . . .

"Adulteress!" he said softly—and his voice was entirely clear.

CHAPTER TWENTY-TWO

"WHAT is happening to him? Elizabeth muttered, warily.

Dr. Leon only shook his head and she stood up to back away from Don Medina. The doctor set his arm about her, and together they stared intently toward the wreck they had created.

Nicholas was laughing once more, and with a sudden flow of energy he freed himself from the tangled folds of his dressing robe. As if it were the most natural thing in the world, he arose to his full height. For a brief space, he busied himself in dusting the heavy brocade, making faint sounds of distaste for its filthy condition.

"Tchk, tchk," he said absently, as he pulled and patted straight the velvet collar and cuffs. When all was to his liking, he turned—and seemed to spy his companions for the first time. "Ah, there you are! I bid you welcome!"

The doctor exhaled deeply—as I did myself at my vantage post above, though for a different reason. Both os us, I knew, had had a momentary wonder whether Nicholas Medina might not, after all, have regained his sanity. Elizabeth still stared uneasily at her husband and asked again, "Charles, what is happening?"

Slowly, Nicholas Medina turned toward his wife. "Happening?" he repeated politely. "Why, what should be happening, Isabella . . ."

"Isabella!" she echoed incredulously, and drew in her breath in a gasp of fear. "Oh, no. . . ."

Now Don Medina stood full-face toward me, and in the flickering torchlight I understood her horror. Dirt-stained though it was, his face was strangely calm—but with a slight, rhythmic twitch. *As he moved forward, he limped.*

"Well, do you like my little workshop, Bartolome?" he asked . . . and even his voice was suddenly different: Older, halting, querulous.

"Oh, dear God!" Dr. Leon muttered, holding Elizabeth behind him quickly.

My brother-in-law's tall figure moved slowly away, beyond my sight through the door crack, and I could follow his progress only by the faces turned toward him. :Why, what ails you, brother?" he was saying. "You seem strangely disconcerted.

"And you, my dear—why so pale? Does this—place disturb you? I had thought the two of you would enjoy the novelty of it." Briefly, he limped back within my vision and gestured with a ghastly chuckle.

"Allow me to conduct you about. There is much of interest here . . ."

Now thoroughly frightened, Elizabeth and Dr. Leon backed slowly away from Don Medina, who had turned to survey the torture chamber with satisfaction. "Why, where are you going, Bartolome?" he said, turning back to the shrinking figures. "Do you not care to see my . . ."

It was the doctor who broke first. Whirling, he tore past my sister and lunged for the staircase. In a flash, the maniacal figure of Nicholas was after him, had grasped and thrown the man violently backward to the floor of the torture chamber. "*Leaving* me, Bartolome?" he asked in a dreadful travesty of surprise.

"God, help me!" I prayed and applied my dagger frantically to the stiff leather thong securing the door. No longer was there time to debate my own security, the need for witnesses; no longer was there time to rouse the castle to aid. In my indecision, I had failed once more. Nicholas Medina was not only mad, but turned violent in his insanity by the taunts of my sister.

Nevertheless, and no matter that she deserved to die, I had no wish for her death to be encompassed by my unfortunate brother-in-law. Sharp though it was and sweet to my hand, the Toledo blade on which I had relied was no match for the thick leather . . . and in my near-sobbing haste, I delayed myself yet further as it slipped from the small cut I had finally achieved and slid about futilely along the strap.

Below me and beyond my sight, Dr. Leon evidently still lay on the stone floor, groaning slightly, while Elizabeth had drawn back in another direction. Don Medina limped after her.

"I am going to torture you, Isabella. I am going to make you suffer for your faithlessness to me," he remarked pleasantly. "Before this day is out, you will be begging me to *kill* you—and relieve you of the agonies of hell into which your husband is about to plunge you."

"No!" I shouted at last. "Hold your hand, Don Medina."

But they heard me not, as the storm broke once more in a full fury of thunder and lightning. Dimly, I heard my sister's scream of fright and glimpsed her moving wildly, evading Don Medina's clutching hands and running for the stairs. His long strides easily overtook her; his great sensitive fingers gripped her shoulders cruelly and forced her to her knees, where she screamed and writhed to free herself, but to no avail. I had had reason to think those delicate hands contained unsuspected power; now insanity had given them an extra strength.

As I cut and slashed at the restraining leather, I shouted over and over . . . but Nicholas and Elizabeth were lost in the tumult of sound they were creating, intensified by the rolling thunder beyond the barred windows.

"Harlot!" he bellowed. *"You will die in agony!"*

Dragging her to her feet, he shook her as limply as a rag doll. "Did you never suspect, my sweet Isabella, that I—your husband—was quite aware of those stolen hours with Bartolome? In the delicious warmth of his bed, did you spare a thought for mine?"

Suddenly, his eyes slid to the left and with a yell he threw Elizabeth from him, plunging from my sight. My sister fell against the hearthstone and lay motionless. I knew not if she were dead, or rendered unconscious when her head struck the cold flags . . . but the shocking sight stayed my hand briefly, and involuntarily I closed my eyes in horror.

What had drawn Nicholas Medina away from his grasp of Elizabeth? It could only be some movement from Dr. Leon—and shortly I saw the doctor scrambling upon the lowest steps. Behind him, Don Medina's avenging form sprang forward and with a mighty heave, had pulled the man backward to sprawl full length upon the floor.

And now, Bartolome . . . my brother . . . my *dearest* brother . . ." Nicholas said with a terrible grin. "Now, I will deal with you."

Dazed, Dr. Leon pulled himself from the floor and attempted to regain some control of the madman. "NICHOLAS!" he shouted compellingly. "It is I—your friend! Charles Leon, Nicholas—CHARLES LEON!"

"There is no escape, Bartolome," Nicholas said, and moved upon the doctor with catlike steps.

In the corner of my eye, it seemed Elizabeth had stirred slightly. Frantically, I returned to my attack upon the thong, and now I ignored the crashing sounds below, nor tried to view what passed, but concentrated on severing the barrier. I cared little what might happen to the doctor, but if Elizabeth were yet living, I must withdraw her from the insane attack of Nicholas Medina—even if that release were only to deliver her into the hangman's hands. Still, that would be better than torture . . .

Below me, Dr. Leon was evading his pursuer; their gasping breaths and thudding footsteps play a cat-and-mouse game back and forth across my vision. As if I had been present, I knew the crashes I heard were sounds of the torture instruments being thrown to the stone floor in Don Medina's path.

With no personal interest in Dr. Leon's safety, I yet felt a responsibility to join him—for the two of us, united, sane and vigorous as we were, might suffice to subdue Nicholas before he turned murderer in his madness.

Spending a small part of my energy, I continued to shout as the stout leather began, at last, to yield to my dagger. If the clamor made no impression on the running figures below me, it might yet serve to rouse servants behind me . . . and at last I thought, above the sounds of the storm, I did hear a faint cry at my back.

"A Medina" I shouted. Rally *Medina* . . . " hoping someone might yet come to my aid.

Once more the adroit figure of Dr. Leon crossed below me, followed by Nicholas Medina. "Why do you run from me, brother," he was saying. "Come, let us examine my toys together . . . perhaps there will be one to please you. Oh no . . ." as the doctor strategically dodged behind a table and overturned it behind him, "do not break my pretty toys!"

Then again they passed from my sight, but I had sensed the doctor was tiring, both from the exertion of his movement and the blow he had suffered on his head. His breath came in sobs, and I heard a sudden protest from Nicholas Medina.

"No—not to that chamber! There is my masterpiece . . .it is not for your vile eyes, Bartolome . . ."

Amid crashing thunder, at long last the strap fell apart and I dashed onto the balcony. My first thought was for Elizabeth: was she dead, or only injured? I paused briefly to reconnoiter; let the doctor care for himself—while he engaged Don Medina's attention, I might be able to remove my sister's body without his knowledge.

A sudden increase in the dim light of the torture chamber told me the doctor had managed to open the barred door in a desperate effort to find another exit. Now his wary footsteps and panting breath, and the cooing voice of Don Medina, withdrew from me a little, and I hastened down the steps toward Elizabeth . . . but had not reached her in my care to pick my way silently through the overturned objects strewn across the floor, when I heard a dreadful scream and thud from the chamber beyond.

"Bartolome—where are you, my brother?" Don Medina's voice said in bewilderment. "Come, you cannot hide from me . . ." I could hear his limping footsteps beyond the door, and to my horror, knew Dr. Leon—for whatever reason—was no more a diversion. Swiftly I retreated, but had only reached the lowest steps of the staircase when the menacing figure of Don Medina appeared in the doorway.

From my witness of the previous course of events, I stayed my steps and moved cautiously, for it seemed that it was only sudden movement that stirred Nicholas to violence. I knew myself to be no match for him physically, nor did I wish to be forced to defend myself for my life against my own brother-in-law by use of the dagger in my hand.

Above and beyond me I could hear rain but definite sounds of activity, and my heart leaped hopefully. Could I but hold Don Medina from further madness, aid would come. I would try the utmost calmness and normalcy. Gently I moved upward a step . . . and another step . . . while he stood staring at me blankly. At my third movement, though, he came forward on a rush. "Ah, I have found you Bartolome . . ."

Instantly I stood still,turning to look down at him with an effect of complete sanity. *There* you are, sir," I said heartily. "In truth, you have given me a fright. We have been searching for you everywhere."

His eyes stared at me, wavered away before the casualness of my tone, and I dared again to retreat a step—but it would not serve. He was forward to me with a great spring, standing at the foot of the staircase with a ghastly smile bearing his even white teeth.

"Will you not return to your bed, sir?" I murmured soothingly. "You are full weary and in need of rest."

Again he peered upward to me, his face falling into a witless non-comprehension, and for a moment I thought I had succeeded. "Yes," he sighed, "I am—tired." With a wavering gesture, his hand went pathetically to his head. "There is a buzzing . . . a hive of bees have found their way through my ears and are moving about in my brain . . . I can smell the sweet clover of their honey . . ." He looked at me piteously and confided, "Clover honey is good with bread . . ."

Almost I had him tamed; standing still on the steps above him and forcing my body to relax, creating by every means I knew, the sense of accustomedness. I stretched out my hand and coaxed him gently. "Will you not come with me now, sir? Lean upon my arm and allow me to conduct you . . ."

His eyes grew dull and vacant. "Yes," he said. "Yes, I am coming.

Then in the outer corridor there were running footsteps and those sounds of alert search I had so long to hear but a short while past—yet now could have cursed for their inopportuneness. Don Medina stiffened and cocked his head listening.

"It is nothing, sir," I urged mildly. Come with me and see for yourself." And as he hesitated upon the steps, I thought to persuade him. Turning, I moved deliberately upward—upward—toward the great door of the torture chamber, thinking he would follow me. Nor did I turn when I heard his whimper of distress behind me, but continued upon my way and hoped to lure him with me.

I had nearly gained the balcony when I heard his steps rush up behind me, and some instinct made me whirl, to throw my arm before my face—but in vain. I saw his eyes blazing at me, saw the poker upraised. I heard his demented voice mutter indistinctly, "And now, for you—Bartolome . . .

while yet you are alive . . .*my ultimate device of torture!:*

Then the poker descended upon my head, and for a space, I knew no more. . .

CHAPTER TWENTY-THREE

ABOVE me was a flickering of torchlight as I opened my eyes. It struck me like a knife and with an involuntary groan, I dropped my lids in protection against the pain . . . then forced them open again dazedly. Was I dreaming—or was this reality?

A figure in black shuffled its way across my view. It held a torch in one hand and chuckled quietly. Again I closed my eyes against the stabbing pain of the light—and felt a breath upon my face. Staring upward, I thought I recognized a distorted caricature of some face I knew. Holding high the flambeau, it leaned over me with a dreadful soft cackle, and nodded a gigantic head topped by a black hood.

"And are you ready now, Bartolome?" it murmured. "Ready to sample my delicious toys . . ." and cackled again.

It is a dream, a nightmare; I will throw it from me . . . but when I sought to raise myself, I was prevented. *Thus it always is with dreams,* I thought fuzzily—and on a sudden, my mind opened to a dreadful clarity. All, *all* returned to me of the past hour.

With my eyes striving to pierce the mists of my mind, I recalled the horrid spectacle of the torture chamber . . . my sister's motionless figure . . . the disappearance of Dr. Leon . . . and the violent madness they had induced in Don Medina.

I remembered my near-success in enticing Nicholas from his lair of blood and death, and those sounds of search that had startled him . . . *but where was I now?*

Struggle as I might, my arms were outflung and secured; I lay on my back, my legs held motionless as my arms. About me I glimpsed a cavernous chamber of rock, upon whose walls my eyes identified a series of ghastly paintings that could only be the creation of a tormented mind. Faces, arms, bodies—strange animals and demons—all writhed and sought to escape the hell-fires painted up-leaping against the rock . . . while cold icicles surrounded pallid suns and moons in a frieze as high as my eye could see.

Overhead—was an arrangement of great wheels and cogs whose meaning my dulled mind could not grasp.

My eye slid to the dark figure moving about. It seemed to stand upon a rocky ledge, somehow separated from the place on which I lay. Swathed in a great black gown, it head hidden in the black hood, it moved from flambeau to flambeau, until it vanished above my strained vision to reappear again on the other side and complete its strange circuit.

With a sudden understanding, all was clear to me: that dark figure could only be Nicholas Medina, garbed in the Inquisition robes of his vile father, Sebastian. Totally mad through the machinations of my sister Elizabeth, his fevered mind had absorbed only the similarity to that earlier tragedy of unchastity and faithlessness.

I could hear his absorbed soft humming, as more and more light sprang into the chamber, and I trembled. Once more it seemed I must be damned whichever way I turned—for to convince him (if I could) that I was *not* his uncle Bartolome but Francis Barnard was still no more than to remind him forcibly of his own untrue wife, Elizabeth.

At length he had completed his task and came once more within my sight. Setting his torch into the last wall holder, he rubbed his hands together in satisfaction and I called to him softly. "Don Medina . . ."

He stopped and turned about uncertainly.

"Don Medina," I said again, most quietly. "Come hither . . ."

Slowly he looked about, searching the walls, throwing his head backward to scan the topmost shadows of the cavern.

"Come!" I whispered, but it was useless, he was too far gone. He merely cackled dementedly once more, and made his way toward me across (I surmised) some bridge connecting the ledge I could see with the plateau on which I lay.

"Do you know where you are, Bartolome?"

"Don Medina—I am Francis Barnard," I said. "Do you not recognize me, sir?"

He paid no attention to my urgent words. "I will tell you where you are, Bartolome. You are about to enter Hell. *Hell, Bartolome!*"

With a deep rolling laugh of enjoyment, he swung away from me and pointed to the wall paintings. "The netherworld," he said. "The infernal region—the abode of the damned—the place of torment." Now he was pointing to the walls beyond my wight, and yelling with satisfaction. "Pandemonium . . . Abaddon . . . Tophet . . .Gehenna . . . Naraka . . ."

His voice had risen to a shriek, then dropped to a quietude more deadly than his clamor.

"The Pit," said Nicholas Medina. Stepping a pace away from me, he pointed upward to the infernal machinery above, ", , , and *The Pendulum!*"

Looking upward, fascinated by his bony forefinger, I could not restrain a gasp . . . for now I saw what my dimmed eyes had only scarce comprehended before among the wheels and cogs: a brass rod centered in the circular ceiling—its end: a crescent of glittering steel about a foot from horn to horn.

This was the "apparatus" my brother-in-law had so casually dismissed upon my arrival at Castle Medina! Now I recalled that dread oscillation, the whining noise I had heard as I followed Catherine in my first traverse of the corridor leading to the crypt.

Immobilized upon the centered stone slab, I looked upon it with mingled dread and fascination. I could visualize, with an inner scream, the swift slashing descent of that keen blade—realize its path must be cunningly devised to slice across the table upon which I lay—yet still admire the arrangement of pulleys, cogs and levers that powered its swing.

"Fate—and fortune," said Nicholas Medina, staring upward in equal fascination. "Fatality and future . . . the prospect of love, the expectation of wealth, the circumstance of luck that makes all possible . . ." His voice dropped a tone. "The razor edge—of destiny," he said mystically. "Thus, the condition of man—bound upon an island from which he can never hope to escape, surrounded by the waiting Pit of Hell—subject to the inexorable Pendulum of fate which must destroy him finally, hurling him into the dark abyss.

For some moments now I had been conscious, through Nicholas Medina's ravings, of faint voices and sounds from beyond the door. Now at last there was a knock, and Catherine's voice cried anxiously, "Nicholas!"

Don Medina paused and turned toward the door; a pathetic look of indecision overspread his face as he listened.

"Nicholas!" she cried again. "Are you there? For God's sake, answer me!"

I held my breath as he wavered, his face turned piteously to his sister's voice—but he said only, "Hush, Bartolome . . .when they have gone, we will play with our toys . . . *alone.*"

Then I knew it was hopeless; gathering every force of lung power I possessed, I shouted, "Catherine—help me! Help me!: Instantly he was upon me, his great hand covering my mouth, and there was silence, in which I heard again Catherine's uncertain voice, calling "Nicholas? Did you call. Are you there?"

Twist as I might, I could not free myself from his smothering hand for a further shout, and at last my mouth was gagged by a strip of cloth he'd found in his pocket.

Then he retreated toward the door, ignoring the furious battering knocks and cries beyond. He bent and seemed to be removing, retrieving, some object . . . and in a second as I strained to look sidewards, I realized he had withdrawn the plank walk that connected the encircling ledge with the stone island on which I was pinioned.

Still I heard Catherine's voice beyond the door, faintly crying "Nicholas—answer me!" I think nothing in my life will ever equal the terror of those moments in which I realized help was at hand—but could not be summoned to my aid because of the gagged and bound position to which I had come!

Meanwhile, Nicholas had limped along the ledge to remove a black cloth from a great lever placed in the floor. It was accompanied by what seemed to be a control wheel, and with a terrible smile, Don Medina placed his hands tightly upon the lever and said, "*Now,*Bartolome . . ."

Vigorously he thrust forward the lever, and above me began again the dreadful grinding noise I had heard upon my arrival at Castle Medina. It had the effect of gigantic clockworks, moving ponderously into motion, and involuntarily my eyes flew upward.

The brass rod trembled and shook; then as my eyes followed its length to the razor-edged crescent, it shivered violently—and abruptly swung downward in a great arc. Despite my faintness as it approached me, I realized it would not strike my body, but only pass in its hissing shriek some few feet above me.

And so it was. Although I had closed my eyes as it swung over me, and only felt the whistling wind of its passage, I could draw breath once more before its return. Once—twice—thrice did it swing down and across my pinioned body, and on its third journey I was so far in command of myself as to observe its entire circuit.

It seemed to approach no more than two or three feet, passing in a line across my chest that must (if it were lower) inevitably expose and sever my heart. Nicholas Medina stood on the encircling ledge, his head following the arc of the pendulum with infantile joy. Finally, rubbing his hands together with satisfaction, he turned to the great wheel beside the pendulum lever and moved it slightly *and above me, with a grinding noise, the brass rod of the pendulum hitched down a notch.*

Now at last I understood the full terror above me! Totally mad and delighting in his toy, my brother-in-law chuckled and rubbed his hands in glee, and skipped with joy—his eyes entirely for the whistling, gleaming slash of the pendulum swinging to and fro above me, and inching downward with his every turn of the wheel.

Down and down it came, to a matter of inches from my body, and the gleaming brilliance of its metal razor in the torchlight had so stupefied and hypnotized me that I lay numb. No longer did I struggle, uselessly, to free myself; instead I followed its appointed path with eyes as detached as my brother-in-law's . . . until at last I felt it brush and slit my shirt.

Then did I yell in horror soundlessly behind the gag, while Nicholas

Medina capered and chortled upon the ledge clapping his hands and bending to and fro, as he watched. Inevitably, when he next set his hand to the wheel, the razor edge would reach my body.

Suddenly, he stopped and stared toward the doorway. Deafened as I was by the noise of the machinery of the pendulum, I had heard nothing, but instead of approaching the wheel once more, he shuffled away and seemed to be listening . . . and twisting my body as best I could, while still shrinking myself as far as possible from the rushing pendulum, I could glimpse a trembling of the great door, as if under attack from violent blows from without.

Now the suspense was well nigh too great to be borne. The door shivered and shook . . . and Nicholas Medina mouthed in terror, turning first as if in flight; then, his eye caught by the flashing metal, shambling back toward the control wheel with a happy smile.

Faintly, beyond the frightful noise within the chamber, I thought I could hear Catherine's voice, anguished and pleading. "Nicholas . . . Nicholas, open the door . . ."

Again, Don Medina shrank back from the entrance and looked at the door, and now, clearly, I could hear Catherine's sweet voice crying, "Make haste, *oh, make haste!*" A mighty succession of blows had nearly conquered the stout wood panels. Indeed, I thought I had glimpsed the edge of an ax blade, and heard myself sobbing with relief.

Above me, on the stone ledge encircling the room, Don Medina limped back and forth in mad distress, whimpering like a child thwarted at play and cringing with every blow at the door. Again and yet again, the bright edge of an ax blade showed through the heave panels, to be wrenched back for further blows, and slowly the thick wood was splintering.

"Nicholas, Nicholas—answer me! Catherine wailed. "Open the door, *open the door . . .*"

Still he wavered above me and still the door resisted in the protesting scream of torn wood—and still the pendulum blade swung back and forth, back and forth—slicing my shirt to ribbons that tore away, were lifted and scattered like snow-flakes as the blade reached its peak and, with a metallic shudder, reversed itself.

I could bear no more; my eyes closed against the pounding of my heart and through the thick folds of the gag I struggled for words. "Our Father Who art in Heaven, Hallowed be Thy name. Thy kingdom come, Thy will be done on earth as it is in Heaven . . . give us this day our daily bread . . . and forgive us our trespasses as we forgive those who trespass against us . . . *Dear God, help me!*" I prayed wildly—and opened my eyes, fearfully, hopefully . . . to see a section of the door panel chopped away, falling inward. Through the jagged space a sturdy arm stretched to fumble for the bolts and withdraw them . . . and simultaneously, Nicholas Medina gave a great cry and leaped for the control wheel.

Now in truth did I know agony of spirit, as the pendulum lowered itself another notch, and rushed downward. Expelling all my breath in the greatest effort possible, I strove instinctively to shrink my body to its least dimension, nor dared to raise my eyes until the hot metallic breath of the blade had passed me by—when half-fainting, I found myself yet alive.

The door opened; Maximilian rushed in with Catherine behind him. Don Medina turned upon the servant with an animal cry of rage, while Catherine shrank against the shattered wood, hands pressed to her mouth in horrified realization of her brother's madness.

And again the pendulum reversed itself with its deadly shudder and swung down to me—and again I braced myself and sucked in my breathe until it had passed, but knew this time I had misjudged its speed and that it had grazed my body. Faintly, I could see the welling drops of blood spring in a line across my chest, while the ghastly blade creaked onward and upward.

"Francis!" Catherine cried in horror, and ran to grapple with the lever. Her tiny hands were unequal to the force needed, but seeing her efforts, Nicholas Medina uttered another howl of rage and attempted to tear himself free from Maximilian.

Bloodied and fainting as I was, this was the moment of supreme agony—for I knew (none better) the insane strength of the man. Could he but break from the servant's hands, Catherine's life would instantly be forfeit—and if so, then let the pendulum be lowered until it sliced me in half, for what would life be without Catherine?

Still, bravely she tugged at the machinery; I could see her sobbing, gathering together her strength to try, and try again . . . while Maximilian wrestled with his master. Don Medina's long arms had reached to encircle the servant's throat, but with a lithe twist of his body, Maximilian had broken the hold and flung his master from him in an effort to gain a breathing spell.

But—the ledge was narrow. Nicholas Medina's huge bulk slid backward, hovered with flailing arms for an instant, then with a terrible echoing cry—*vanished downward* . . .

Once more the pendulum grazed past my face, and absorbed in the dreadful spectacle before me, I had failed to prepare for its passage. I felt its razor-edge across my chest . . . and merciful blackness encompassed me . . .

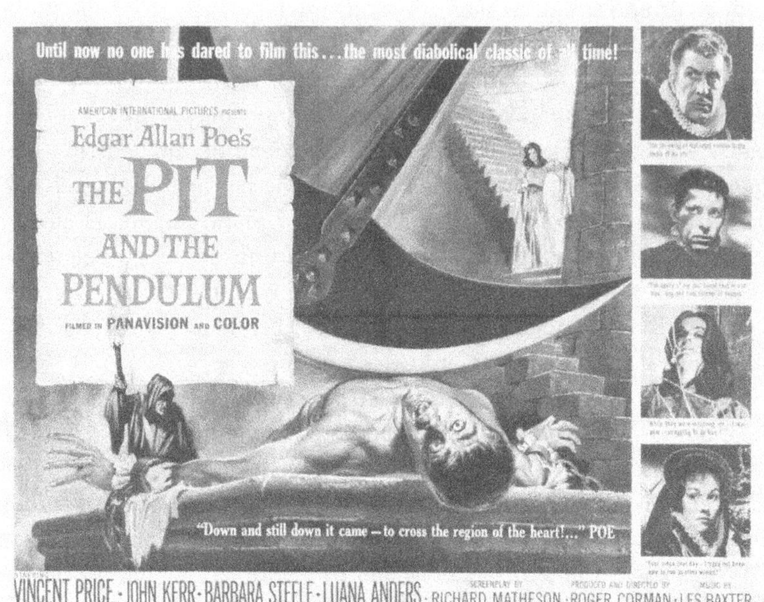
Until now no one has dared to film this... the most diabolical classic of all time!
AMERICAN INTERNATIONAL PICTURES presents
Edgar Allan Poe's
THE PIT
AND THE
PENDULUM
FILMED IN PANAVISION AND COLOR
"Down and still down it came — to cross the region of the heart!..." POE
VINCENT PRICE · JOHN KERR · BARBARA STEELE · LUANA ANDERS · RICHARD MATHESON · ROGER CORMAN · LES BAXTER

CHAPTER TWENTY-FOUR

GRATEFULLY, my ears absorbed silence—blessed silence. My cheeks felt a dampness—of tears; my nose was filled with the faint perfume of roses that reminded me of delectable women; my eyes opened—to the pansy-brown gaze of Catherine Medina.

"He is alive," she said. "Oh, thank God! Maximilian, make haste to free him . . ."

Above me, Maximillian's face hovered intently. As he severed the gag with a careful knife stroke and took it from my parched mouth, I could see the odious pendulum once more quiet and withdrawn to its highest position of rest . . .glistening, gleaming, deadly. With a shudder I closed my eyes, and felt the bindings at my arms and legs removed.

Gentle hands moved across my chest, stanching the wound and pulling my torn shirt together, and I tried my limbs with an involuntary groan for their stiffness.

"Be at peace, Mr. Barnard," Catherine's voice murmured. "It is over." She caught her breath in a sob. "All over . . ."

I looked at her anxious small face, bent mistily above me. "You called me 'Francis' before," I said hoarsely.

Her eyelids fluttered. "It—was ever a favorite name of mine, sir."

Maximilian's concerned face bent above me now. "Can you rise, sir?" he asked. "Will you take my arm?"

"Yes," I said, and pulled myself up and off the stone table with his aid. Each movement was a torment to me, but in the sweetness of freedom, I ignored the pain. "Don Medina . . ." I said, remembering. "He thought I was your uncle Bartolome . . . "

Catherine's face paled again. "Hush," she said. "It is over; my dear lord, think no more on it."

Bemused by her loving words, I stood straightly and clinging to Maximilian's arm. At last I saw the full pan of Don Medina's "apparatus". We stood upon a stone island, rearing itself from a circular stone moat and connected to the encircling ledge by a movable plan bridge. Maximilian's sober eyes met mine in a glance of sick comprehension as I finished my survey.

"Sir—let us go," he said quietly. "Can you walk—or will you let me carry you?"

But although my legs were stiff, I found them still ready to obey my commands. "I can walk," I told him, and with Catherine preceding us, we made our way slowly across the planks toward the door . . . but it was only as we traversed the bridge that I realized the full horror of the chamber.

Looking down, I saw The Pit of which Don Medina had spoken in his madness—and deep within it, his sightless eyes staring up at us in the glaze of death, lay Dr. Leon. I looked quickly ahead, but Catherine had passed on, to stand with bowed head at the doorway; she saw not our discovery. . . . Nor that other figure, lying crumpled beyond the doctor.

In death, Nicholas Medina's handsome face was calm again. Maximilian's arm trembled beneath my hand, and I pressed it reassuringly. "Better so, better so," I murmured for his ears alone. "God rest his soul, poor fellow . ."

Slowly we moved on from the inner to the outer chamber, and here was the moment I dreaded. The storm still raged in its fury beyond the high barred windows; the turbulent ocean spray still swept up to beat its way in to Sebastian Medina's "playroom." All was in the wildest disarray, following Dr. Leon's attempt to evade Don Medina . . . but when I had forced my eye to the stone hearth, *I saw no female figure!*

"Where is she?" I asked, ere I thought. *"Where is Elizabeth?"*

Catherine and Maximillian looked at each other, and would have drawn me on without answer, but I stood still. "Oh, *I* am not mad," I said quietly. "It *was* she . . .it was Elizabeth, all the time.

"Do you not understand? It was a plot, between herself and the doctor. The body in the coffin was not Elizabeth, but some unfortunate roadside woman, whom the doctor drugged to provide a corpse.

Catherine drew a horrified breath, but Maximilian's eyes merely regarded me gravely.

"You—are not surprised?" I asked him, and unwillingly, he shook his head.

"I—did not *know,*" he told me, "but sometimes I thought there seemed—too close an understanding between the mistress and Dr. Leon. And the secret passages have long been rumored in the kitchen quarters, sir, though no one knew where they lay."

"Elizabeth found the drawings for them, " I replied, "and conceived a plan to use them in driving Nicholas Medina insane—because his testament appointed Dr. Leon as guardian for the estate. Maria was right, and Nicholas—it *was* Elizabeth's own voice they heard. And then—tonight. . . ."

"Do not think of it!" Catherine pleaded, and would have drawn me to the staircase. "Do not think of it now, Francis."

"But we must think of it," I said more strongly. "For where *is* Elizabeth? In his madness, your poor brother threw her away from him. She fell and struck her head; she lay on the cold hearthstone, but whether dad or unconscious I do not know—and now her body is gone . . ."

Slowly, I forced myself to gaze about the room, from one instrument of torture to another, and at last, lit by vivid lightning I saw the Iron Box with the barred window.

Staring sightlessly from that "toy" of her long-dead father-in-law, which she had sought to use in her own vile plot . . . the strangled body of my sister Elizabeth had finally come home to rest by the hands of the husband she had maddened to death.

THE END

James H. Nicholson, the president of American International Pictures, poses with Vincent Price and producer and director Roger Corman at California Studios

The Making of The Pit and the Pendulum

Cobwebs, spriders and a soda during a break

THE MAKING OF THE PIT AND THE PENDULUM

by

LAWRENCE FRENCH

In the fall of 1960, American-International Pictures was basking in the glory of their first legitimate movie 'classic.' *House of Usher* had become not only a tremendous smash at the box-office, but also a genuine critical success. Naturally, the top men at AIP, James H. Nicholson and Samuel Z. Arkoff, immediately began thinking about other Poe stories they could adapt for an even scarier follow-up that would contain all the elements that had made *House of Usher* such a big hit.

According to Roger Corman, the choice for a second film came down to two of Poe's best stories: *The Masque of the Red Death* and *The Pit and the Pendulum.* "What happened," relates Corman, "is Jim and Sam asked me to do another Poe picture. At first I wanted to adapt *The Masque of the Red Death*, because I always felt it was one of Poe's finest stories, but I ultimately didn't choose it because I saw certain similarities between Poe's story and Ingmar Bergman's *The Seventh Seal* (released in America in 1958). Both films were set in the Middle Ages and both had scenes of Death personified, so I felt if I did *Masque of the Red Death* people might think I had copied from Ingmar Bergman. But I had always liked Poe's *The Pit And The Pendulum* as well, so I said to Jim and Sam, 'All right, let's make that one instead. I also felt that the climax could be visually very exciting. That was how we ended up making *The Pit And The Pendulum* as the second Poe film. But at that point it wasn't evident that I was going to embark on a whole series of Poe pictures. I simply thought, 'Now there will be two Poe films, instead of one.' "

Roger Corman (holding pendulum) prepares the crew for the climax of the picture

Once again, Arkoff disputes Corman's version of events, saying, "In the first place, it was Jim and I who decided on making *The Pit And The Pendulum* as the next Poe film because it was a lot more graphic, and in the second place, *Masque of the Red Death* would have needed a dancing troupe that would have been quite expensive. In all those early Poe pictures we had relatively few actors, so when we finally did make *Masque of the Red Death* we went to the UK where it would be less expensive to do it."

In retrospect, Arkoff's point about the dancing troupe is well taken, since if Corman had made *Masque* as his second Poe film, it seems quite likely it would have suffered from an inadequate budget as well as a very tight shooting schedule. Two years later, when Corman did make *Masque of the Red Death* in England, he not only had the advantage of a greater budget but also the luxury of a five-week shooting schedule for the first time in his career. *

---

*An interesting side note that connects Corman and Matheson to movies that are among their best work in terror filmmaking was the real life horror of president John F. Kennedy being assassinated (on November 22, 1963). Corman was shooting *The Masque of the Red Death* in England with Vincent Price when they heard the awful news. At the same time in California, Richard Matheson was driving home after a game of golf with Jerry Sohl, and was being tailgated by a unknown driver who became the inspiration for Matheson's short story *Duel.* That story, in turn, became the basis for the famed TV-movie that saw Hollywood first take notice of director Steven Spielberg.

It's also fascinating to speculate on what Matheson might have done had he been assigned *The Masque of the Red Death* as his second Poe film. It seems probable he would have added more thrills and terror content than the more philosophical approach Corman eventually opted to explore when he made his penultimate Poe movie. Matheson remembered he didn't have a say in choosing the second Poe story, remarking, "They probably told me, but *The Pit and the Pendulum* was just a short story, so I really had to write an original screenplay for that one. I tried to use as much from the original as I could, but Poe's story is very short, so I just used it for the last scene of the film, where John Kerr is strapped underneath the blade. Other than that, it was a totally original plot. In fact, I had developed an outline for a novel I was starting to work on called *House of the Dead*. So when they wanted me to write *The Pit and the Pendulum,* I used the outline for *House of the Dead* as the basis for my screenplay."

When Corman and Matheson met to discuss the script for *Pit and the Pendulum*, they both realized they would have to come up with something new and different, yet at the same time they wanted to adhere to the key elements that had made *House of Usher* such a success. By adapting a new Poe story, Matheson had the luxury of working in the same milieu as *House of Usher*, but his creative freedom wasn't as restricted as if he were writing a

Director Roger Corman consulting with actor John Kerr and Oscar winning cinematographer Floyd Crosby on the torture Chamber set of The Pit and the Pendulum.

For his part, Corman deliberately wanted to start *The Pit and the Pendulum* in a way similar to *House of Usher*. "A young man approaches a the door. After being refused entrance, they are led into the house, but are not introduced to Vincent Price right away. I also used a similar introduction to how they meet Vincent Price in both pictures. In *House of Usher* as Mark Damon approaches the door to his room, I have it open quickly, and Vincent Price comes through the door. I varied that in *The Pit and the Pendulum*, by having Vincent unexpectedly come through a door from the right, in a very sharp, close shot."

Corman also realized that the second film would have to contain more Matheson and less Poe. "*The Pit and the Pendulum* was actually one of the most difficult of the Poe pictures to write," Corman declared, "because Poe's original story had almost no characterization in it at all, whereas in *The Fall of the House of Usher* there was at least enough characterization to build a screenplay out of the story. So although we tried, whenever we could, to be faithful to Poe, we had to vary them to a large extent; otherwise, the picture would only be 25 minutes long. Poe's original story was about a man in a room being tortured during the Spanish Inquisition, and we simply utilized that by having John Kerr come to Vincent Price's castle and then put him under the pendulum for the climax of the film. You could think of it as our creating a two-act prologue that leads up to the third act—which would be the actual Poe story. But in creating the first two acts, Dick Matheson attempted to use concepts and themes that Poe developed in his other stories. For example, the idea of Vincent Price walling up his unfaithful wife was something Poe had used in his other stories, particularly in *The Cask of Amontillado*. So, although we were inventing a story of our own, we generally tried to maintain a consistency of thought towards Poe's work, by incorporating similar ideas taken from his other stories."

Matheson's final script is dated December 12, 1960, and Corman began filming on January 4, 1961, not in the studio but on location. Corman recalls, "For the first day of shooting I took a skeleton crew down to the ocean at Palo Verdes to shoot John Kerr's arrival at the castle and then we came back to shoot the rest of the movie on studio interiors (once again at California Studios). My theory was, except for brief scenes of travel, to never photograph anything that wasn't built in the studio, so for the opening where we see John Kerr's carriage approaching the castle, I felt the best thing to do was to show it against a stark ocean background. My reason for that was because water has a very dreamlike quality, and although the ocean is reality, if you follow strict Freudian beliefs, it's still highly symbolic. There are various qualities we associate with the ocean—it symbolizes certain natural powers and forces. It's where we all came from originally, so I think it can have a number of meanings that relate it to the unconscious."

With the addition of some beautifully executed matte paintings, the Palo Verdes coast stands in admirably for Spain's rugged Costa de Cantabria, west of San Sebastian. In his script, Matheson never specifies the exact location of the castle, but it would most likely be somewhere near the medieval Spanish town of Santillana Del Mar and the wondrous caves of Altamira, since a short ways inland there are two Spanish cities—Medina de Pomar and León—which probably gave Matheson the inspiration for the names of two of his leading characters. Matheson also established the time and general setting of the story in his opening narration, which Corman subsequently decided to eliminate:

FRANCIS BARNARD: By late afternoon upon that autumn day in the year of our Lord 1546, the coach, which I had hired that morning, was far away from San Sebastian. Perhaps it was prophetic that my first view of the Castle Medina should have come just as darkness was descending upon the Spanish countryside. Certainly it was disconcerting to have the driver refuse to take me to the castle door.

Forman explained: "We had an opening narration spoken by John Kerr, that told the audience we were in 16th-century Spain, but I deliberately decided to cut it because I thought the film stood on its own and didn't need an explicit narration saying when and where it was taking place." Instead, Corman filmed the whole opening prologue as written by Matheson, but as if it were a silent movie. We see Mr. Barnard's arrival at the castle, the coachman's refusal to take him any further, and his approach to the front door of the castle, all done without any dialogue.

This silent opening scene was tremendously effective in establishing the gloom and isolation that the story demanded. Luckily, Daniel Haller was able to convince Universal's resident matte artist, Albert Whitlock, to execute the paintings in his brief periods of time off from his major studio assignments. We see Castle Medina perched on a cliff amid a cloud-filled sky, and it appears that Whitlock modeled his painting on the famous 12th century Alcazar castle in Segovia, Spain, with its ship-like prow and it's many towers and turrets.

When Vincent Price first read the script he was especially pleased, since he felt Matheson had managed to retain the flavor of what he regarded as Poe's most fearsome story. Indeed, Price pointed out that almost every element of human fear is utilized in both story and script, including fear of heights, rats, insanity, enclosed places, ghosts, premature burial and death. "And," Price added, "the thought of being tortured by that enormous razor-sharp blade." Price also knew that for this second film, the part of Nicholas Medina was being written specifically for him. "Richard Matheson knew I was being cast in it," said Price, "but the trouble was, Poe wrote very short stories and we had to make a long movie, which isn't easy. *The Pit and the Pendulum* is what—only 20 pages long? So the story had to be expanded. How did the guy get into the pit? What got the characters into the settings was part of the problem that Matheson had to deal with. You can't just go into the film and have a man being tortured under a pendulum—although that is exactly what Poe did in his short story."

As Price notes, Poe's story starts with an unnamed narrator being tortured in the depths of a dungeon in Toledo, during the last gasps of the Spanish Inquisition. That meant, besides creating an original plot, Matheson had to come up with all the appropriate names for his cast of characters. Luckily, he could turn to Poe for inspiration, since in *The Fall of the House of Usher*, Poe cites *The Inquisition Directorium* as being one of Roderick Usher's favorite books. That volume was a treatise written by the Spanish Dominican cleric, Nicolas Eymeric of Gironne, who became the Inquisitor General of Aragon in 1357. Eymeric completed *The Inquisition Directorium* in 1378, but it wasn't widely printed until 1403, four years after his death. It went on to become one of the most widely used procedural texts during the Spanish Inquisition and cited many of the magical manuscripts Nicolas had confiscated from accused sorcerers and witches.

Other character names appear to have been taken from Spanish historical figures of the period. Isabella and Catherine, for instance, were well-known Spanish Queens of the 16th century, while another real life Spaniard, Bartolomé Medina, was a famed Catholic theologian who also lived during the fifteen hundreds. "I usually tried to find the kinds of names that felt appropriate to the story," says Matheson, "and I'd also use 18th and 19th century words. But my biggest mistake in *The Pit and the Pendulum* was having John Kerr calling Vincent Price 'Don Medina' throughout the movie. That is totally wrong, but at the time I didn't know it. In Spain they address a person as 'Don' and then his first name, not his last name. So what he should have been saying was 'Don Nicholas.' But it's something I missed at the time, and if I ever watch the movie now, it's a mistake that still bothers me." *

Filming the descent of Nicholas to the crypt. Cinematographer Floyd Crosby made effective use of spotlights to simulate candlelight in the castle's many dark and secret passageways where rats and spiders dwell in the darkness.

*Presumably, when the film was dubbed in Spain, the Spanish voice actors corrected this mistake. If not, the film probably got unintentional laughs from audiences in Spain and Latin America.

It seems odd that the erudite Vincent Price, who had traveled to both Spain and Mexico, never picked up on Matheson's mistake. However, Price never had to say any of the inaccurate lines. That task fell to the hapless John Kerr, whose performance was in earnest but was heavily criticized. Matheson himself called Kerr "as stiff as a board."

However, the acting in *The Pit and the Pendulum* was actually a step up from the previous film, but was still mostly unremarkable. In defending his casting choices, Corman said, "I took those people because they were good actors and although they were trained in the modern idiom rather than

a more classical acting style, I tried to integrate their acting into the basic framework of the film. I think it was partially successful, and as with all creative work, I think it's possible to say it was not completely successful."

Another improvement that was quite apparent was the more lavish look Corman was able to achieve on *The Pit and the Pendulum*, since AIP agreed to provide a bigger budget totaling nearly $300,000. "The physical look and style did improve," Corman remarked, "because AIP was willing to give me a little bit more money. We also deliberately went for a more luxurious look, because the setting was the castle of a Spanish nobleman, whereas in *House of Usher*, we were in a private house in New England. We also had a habit of saving the sets from one picture to the next. That is, when you break a set down into it's components and into flats, they all go into the scene docks at the studio. So when we came to do *The Pit and the Pendulum*, (production designer) Danny Haller was able to not only build new units, but also take the flats out from *House of Usher* and add on to them. We would repaint them, rearrange them and so on, but they were the same units we had used before. So each succeeding Poe film got a little bit bigger, without that much greater expense. It was as if a little boy had a set of blocks, and he was able to combine one set of blocks, with another set."

Naturally, Corman and Haller wanted the stand-out set to be the pendulum room, where the climax of the story takes place. According to AIP's publicity, Haller did meticulous research and found that a real pendulum was actually used during the Spanish and German inquisitions. When asked about his "research," Haller laughed and said, "What research? That was all overblown, because what we did really had nothing to do with history or architecture. In fact, we had furniture from so many different periods mixed together, if we got something accurate it was usually by mistake. What we did for the pendulum though, was to make it as a kind of a clock, but in reality it would never have worked. We just put up a bunch of gears, as in Chaplin's *Modern Times.* There are shots of the gears going around, but that was done on the floor of the stage with everything painted black above it, so the background just falls off. Floyd Crosby was very good at shooting those things. Where we just had chicken wire, he didn't put light on it, or else he'd fuzz it out around the edges. Doing all that was a lot of fun."

Walking onto the pendulum room set impressed Vincent Price, who commented, "I think Danny was the first person to ever use a complete sound stage. He went right up to the ceiling and removed the catwalks, which gave the set an enormous sense of depth and height." Haller added, "We made the pendulum room really dark, because it was really just a sound stage where we painted everything black. We built everything as high as we could, and all the trusses, and the beams that held up the ceiling—which was about 50 feet high—we painted them all black. Then I had a friend who was a scenic artist come over to paint all the murals on the pendulum room walls, showing the hooded penitents."

Once again Haller rented most of the set pieces from Universal, and had them trucked over to California Studios. "We had to get oversize permits to carry all the sets on the freeway," says Haller. "It was like moving a house. I remember we had several pieces that were originally used for Stanley Kubrick's *Spartacus.* The stone platform John Kerr is strapped to was a Roman burial tomb they had made for *Spartacus.* Then we got a lot of the gargoyles from the Goldwyn Studio and all the torture devices were rented from prop houses."

Despite Haller's claims to the contrary, Corman says "Danny did quite a bit of research. So when we went to the prop houses to rent the set decorations, we tried to get objects that made the sets look as accurate as possible—within the confines of our limited budget. I was very much a believer in what we called 'articulation of the surface'—which was to fill the surface of the set with as many objects as we could get, such as antique furniture with ornate carvings, paintings, statues, candelabra and so forth."

For the pendulum room itself, Haller started construction about a week before shooting and found his crew of plasterers was not working quickly enough. "We started with about ten plasterers doing all the work on the walls," says Haller, "and we had five carriers, the guys who would walk up and give them the plaster. After the first day, we weren't getting enough work done, so I told the construction foreman, 'This isn't going to work out.' Well, there was one guy who was doing most of the work, named Mueller, a German guy who was from MGM. So I said, 'If he wants to work 20 hours, we'll put him on 20 hours.' So we had five guys carrying the plaster for him, and he was just splashing it all over the walls. It was a huge job, going up to the ceiling, and he did it all by himself! In the end, he got some astronomical check, because he was doing it all on overtime and I hadn't cleared it with Roger. When I finally told Roger we had fired the crew and this guy had done the entire job, Roger said, 'You did the right thing.' I never had to clear something like that with Roger if I knew I was right, because although it still had to go through AIP, I always knew Roger would back me up 100 percent." (AIP's publicity claimed 12,000 pounds of plaster were used to make the sets.)

Amazingly, Haller says that other than the pendulum room and a few specialty sets, most of the hallways and rooms were thrown together only a few days before shooting. "We'd have liked to have built everything new, but you just couldn't do it on those budgets," admitted Haller. "So I started a couple of days beforehand and I'd get with the grips and just construct the sets with units we knew we had on hand. I didn't do that many drawings. I'd just go down and put a chalk line on the floor and we'd take the stock units we had rented and I'd say, 'Put this here, and put that one over there.' The construction foreman and his crew would assemble them, then the electricians would know what we were doing and Floyd would know not to put lights on something that had holes in it."

Corman says Haller would sketch all the sets in some detail, but totally supported his off-the-cuff manner of working. "If a set is supposed to be 20 feet long, it makes no true difference if it only goes out 19 feet," Corman declared. "It's not tied to any posts or anything to support a second floor; it's just a backdrop, really. Also, the set will change with every lens you use anyway. And one of the reasons Danny was able to make things work without being totally accurate was because we were re-using existing units. So if a set was anywhere near what we wanted, we would simply use it over again. Then, after doing that, I went over to 20th Century-Fox, and they had this big drafting department, drawing up intricate plans for all the sets. I said, 'Why?' This isn't a house that's going to stand, we know roughly what the set is going to be like so a sketch is truly good enough."

After toiling with Corman for five years on his black-and-white quickie productions, cameraman Floyd Crosby was inspired to do some of his best color cinematography to date, once he saw the elaborate sets Haller had assembled. "When we started to do the Poe pictures," Crosby told *American Cinematographer's* Herb Lightman, "Roger became much more interested in the camera, because we had sets that were exceptionally well designed. They were bigger and better, and that allowed us more interesting opportunities for camera moves. Of course, the bigger the set, the more lights that have to be rigged, all of which takes time. Sometimes we would get all set to shoot and then get a better idea. In the pendulum sequence, for example, we originally rigged the lights high up on the stage, but when we were ready to shoot we realized that making the shadow of the pendulum cut across the figures (on the wall murals) would be more effective. We had to stop and re-set the lights at a lower angle so the dramatic shadow (cast by the swinging pendulum) would not be lost in the depths of the set."

Crosby's expert skill at lighting both the sets and actors in an appropriate low-key format resulted in the film's mesmerizing camera style. "The improvement in camerawork was a development of my own technique," says Corman. "On each subsequent picture I gained a little bit more information as to what I could do. There was also the fact that the picture was fairly dialogue-heavy, with a limited number of sets. That could easily have gotten me into the trap of a rather static film. If you have a 117-page script and 90 pages of it are people talking in rooms, it's very possible to shoot a picture that's just talking heads. So I was determined to use all the cinematic devices I could think of to make the picture more visual. I used a lot of moving camera and a lot of camera angles in order to get as much movement and scope as possible into the film. And on some of the fast pans and shock effects, I would under-crank the camera, so it would move quicker—to give a sense of excitement and also a slight sense of unreality."

The Pit and the Pendulum also saw one of the Poe series recurring trademarks burst into full flower: the use of hundreds of red candles. Floyd Crosby said, "Corman always wanted to have a lot of candles. He thought they were very effective, but he gave me complete freedom in lighting the films."

Hearing Crosby's statement, Corman laughed and said, "As a matter of fact on one of the later Poe films the prop man told me I had the all-time record for the number of candles used in a picture!" (According to AIP's publicity hype, prop man Dick Rubin had 2,000 red candles especially made for *Pit and the Pendulum.*) Corman went on to say, "In terms of the technicalities of the lighting, I left that totally up to Floyd. It would have been very presumptuous of me to start discussing how he was going to light the sets, and I had complete faith in his abilities. He was able to light the set very well, and do it very quickly. It's not that difficult to get a good cameraman if the cameraman has hours to set up each shot. It's not difficult to get a cameraman who works quickly. He just sets up a few lights and says he's ready to shoot. But to get somebody to work quickly and who does fine work is very unusual."

One of the most significant changes Corman made to Matheson's script was in the film's effective twist ending. Elizabeth's scheme to stage her own death has succeeded so well, even her own brother believes her to be dead. Thus, in a supreme irony, Elizabeth faces, in reality, the agonizing death she faked to deceive her husband.

As originally written by Matheson, after Nicholas falls into the pit, he does not die, but regains consciousness. Then, "suddenly, his mind clears and he remembers everything. He tries to get up; cannot." He says:

> NICHOLAS: (horrified) Elizabeth. What have I done to you?
> (beat) *What have I done to you?*
>
> CLOSE UP - ELIZABETH

Her face contorted with horror, her mouth bitter so that she can only make a gagging noise. CAMERA PULLS BACK SLOWLY to include the barred window, then the iron box into which she has been placed by the demented Nicholas. CAMERA KEEPS PULLING BACK and now UPWARD until we see the whole of the torture chamber. Francis, Catherine and Maximilian go out. The door is shut and locked. Off screen the surf. Thunder. Lightning.

Corman changed this by adding a line that emphasizes Elizabeth's fate. When Catherine, Francis and Maximillian exit the torture chamber, Catherine locks the door and firmly says, "No one will ever enter this room again!" * Corman then swish-pans over to Elizabeth staring out from within the iron maiden, as the screen irises-in on Elizabeth's eyes, open wide in horror.

---

* This line echoes Nicholas's earlier pronouncement (in shot #180) that "No one will ever enter this room, again," after he has locked the door to Elizabeth's vandalized room.

Explaining why he changed the ending, Corman said, "When I was working out the visualization for the final film, I felt it was sharper and faster to do it the way I filmed it. So once Vincent fell into the pit, the choice of whether he lived a few seconds and said, 'Elizabeth, what have I done to you?' or whether Vincent died immediately, it probably seemed to me to be faster to have him fall and die, and then swish-pan straight to Elizabeth's eyes staring out, and end on that. I felt it was a more effective and shocking way to do it. I was still staying within the spirit of the script, but I was simply trying to make it a little bit more visual."

Matheson added that his twist ending was, "the sort of thing I would usually come up with and Roger would take it and elaborate on it—that's what a good director should do. But the basic idea was still the same."

For the admirers of Vincent Price, the feverish highlight of the script comes in shots #393 — 407, when the now deranged Nicholas asks Mr. Barnard, "Do you know where your are, Bartolome?" Price goes on to declaim Matheson's speech in his best 'larger-than-life' acting manner, expertly intoning each word as Corman follows Matheson's script precisely, using rhythmic cutaways to the wall paintings, thereby perfectly matching Matheson's rhythmic dialogue:

All dialogue cut from the final film is shown in italics

SERIES OF SHOTS — THE WALL PAINTINGS
Depicting the aspects of Hell. (Nicholas' words match each painting).

NICHOLAS (as SEBASTIAN):
Do you know where you are, Bartolome?
I will tell you where you are.
(beat) You are about to enter Hell.
Hell...Bartolome.
The netherworld.
The infernal region.
Abode of the damned.
The place of torment.
Pandemonium.
Abbaddon.
Tophet.
Gehenna.
Naraka.
The Pit... and the Pendulum.
Fate - and fortune. Fatality and future.
Prospect. Expectation. Circumstance.
The razor edge - of destiny.

Thus, the condition of man - bound upon an island from which he can never hope to escape.

Surrounded by the waiting pit of Hell. Subject to the inexorable pendulum of fate...

Which must destroy him finally - *hurling him into the dark abyss.*

Since many of the names Matheson has used for Hell are no longer familiar, here is a guide to their meaning:

Pandemonium: The abode of all demons; In *Paradise Lost,* Milton's name for the capitol of Hell.

Abaddon: Hebrew name for the leader of the demon locusts that appear in the ninth chapter of Revelation; A place of destruction, the depths of hell; the Angel of the bottomless pit, a destroyer, whose name in Greek is Apollyon (who appears in *The Pilgrim's Progress*).

Tophet: Place in the valley of Hinnom, where children were sacrificed to the Canaanite–Phoenician deity, Moloch; A place of punishment for the wicked after death.

Gehenna: A pre-Christian Hell, where the wicked would writhe in eternal pain; Any place of extreme torment or suffering; The valley of the son of Hinnom, outside of Jerusalem, near Mt. Zion.

Naraka: In Hinduism, a place of torment for the spirits of the wicked.

Matheson recalled reading these lines out loud while he was writing the script to see how they would play when recited by Vincent Price. "Those kinds of words were very carefully chosen," revealed Matheson. "I got them right out of a thesaurus and the reason I'd say them out loud was to get the correct rhythm and cadence and make sure they didn't blur into each other. I carefully sculpted every word, to make it sound just right. That way it would play better for the actors."

Although only three lines were cut from the above speech, many other larger cuts in the dialogue were made throughout the script. Notable among them was in shot #70 where Nicholas goes into more vivid detail about his father's career as an Inquisitor:

NICHOLAS: This was my father's world, Mr. Barnard. *A world of pain and – bestial cruelty – in which my father served the State – by torturing others. You were right – he was degraded. Mad. Inflicting physical agony was all he lived for. The shrieking of – mutilated victims was the music of his life.*

This speech was filmed but subsequently cut in the editing and a portion of it still appears in the movie's trailer. Strangely enough, the line "The shrieking of mutilated victims was the music of his life" was also used prominently in the film's ad campaign under pictures of Vincent Price.

In shots #346 — 349 a long speech by Elizabeth was severely trimmed. It spelled out in much greater detail how she and Dr. Leon planned their duplicitous crimes:

ELIZABETH: Now you are exactly as I want you, Nicholas – *gibbering and helpless. And now your dear old friend, the doctor, will, according to your testament, become the guardian of your wealth. My wealth. My poor – stupid husband. ...(Ghoulishly) Did you enjoy the sight of that woman we put into my casket, Nicholas? ...You never knew about the secret passages, did you dear Nicholas. I found your father's drawing for them.*

Other significant cuts occur in these scenes:

Shots # 166 — 170: Mr. Barnard overhears Catherine and Dr. Leon talking, as Catherine says she has always sensed something wrong about Elizabeth. Mr. Barnard then expresses his anger at being continually misled ever since his arrival at the castle.

Shot #181: Dr. Leon and Mr. Barnard discuss who could have played the harpsichord, with Dr. Leon suggesting Maria may have been the culprit.

Shots # 257 — 258: Mr. Barnard explains to a surprised Catherine that he hardly even knew his sister.

A line that was changed by Vincent Price occurs in shot #19 after we hear Nicholas testing the pendulum. Matheson's script has Nicholas explaining the noise by saying simply, "an apparatus, Mr. Barnard." Price has penciled in an additional line on his script, "that must be kept in constant repair." Corman notes, "That was a line Vincent added that could be taken a little bit humorously, but I wanted to introduce the sound of the pendulum early on, without saying exactly what it was, just to let the audience know subliminally that there is something happening here. It was a way of setting the audience up for what they will eventually see in the climax of the picture, the actual pendulum."

On January 24, 1961, the final day of shooting, Corman managed to shoot the entire pendulum room sequence that covers over 15 pages in Matheson's script. "I remember we shot the whole pendulum sequence in less than a day," maintains Corman, "because after I finished principal photography, there was still an hour or so before we went into overtime. So I got on a Chapman crane with the camera operator and said, 'Let's just move this crane all over the set.' I hadn't planned any of the shots; I just photographed anything that looked good to me: the moving shadows of the pendulum, or the magnificent murals Danny Haller had painted on the studio walls. Then, later on, I figured I'd be able to use all the different shots when I was cutting the scene together. In fact, we spent a fair amount of time cutting that scene—trying it many different ways—and using every technique I could think of to make it work."

Corman revealed that the pendulum room set occupied a whole sound stage at Producers studio, and to make the set look bigger for the long shots, they once again utilized matte paintings by Albert Whitlock. To accomplish this the camera was mounted at the far end of the stage and Crosby shot the live-action set with an extreme wide-angle lens. When the live-action plate was combined with Whitlock's painted extensions both above and below the real set, the illusion of a cavernous abyss below the pendulum was seamlessly achieved.

Once shooting had wrapped, Corman paid especially close attention to the sound effects he would need to complete the realistic illusion of a 16th-century castle with its subterranean torture chamber. Most important were the grating and clanking noises of the pendulum itself, along with the eerie harpsichord music that would be heard echoing throughout the upper rooms of the castle. Kay Rose, the film's sound editor, went on to win an Academy Award in 1984 for Mark Rydell's *The River* and surprisingly enough, AIP actually submitted her work for Academy Awards consideration in 1961, despite its having very little chance of getting a best sound nomination against such big-budgeted stereo films as *West Side Story* and *The Guns of Navarone.*

Corman related that he would always discuss with the sound editor the type of sound effects he was looking for during the final mixing of the dialogue, music and effects tracks. "That way I could control which elements I wanted during the final dubbing of the film," explains Corman. "So I would be there every moment of the mixing, to personally supervise the integration of the sound effects and how they would be used in the soundtrack of the film. And all the different off-screen noises, like the harpsichord and the pendulum were done quite deliberately, to indicate something going on beyond what you were actually seeing onscreen. It served to let the audience know that they were in a world in which the visual was only one aspect. It was also a way of playing with audience expectations. We raised the possibility that there are supernatural events going on, and then gradually we begin to suspect that it is not supernatural, but that something terrible has taken place here." In its submission to the Academy, AIP claimed the final sound effects were achieved by using sounds of sixteen different intensities and pitches, including windmills, blow torches, rail clicks and ratchets. These were speeded up, slowed down, echoed, squeezed and stretched to achieve the desired final effect on the soundtrack.

Barbara Steele in costume for her role as Elizabeth Medina outside of stage 9 at California Studios, formerly owned by Charles Chaplin.

Corman would also have a meeting with composer Les Baxter to give him his thoughts on where he wanted to place music in the film. "I would show Les the first cut of the picture," says Corman, "and discuss with him the type of music we were going to have, the feeling I was looking for and where I wanted it to go. Then Les would go and write it totally on his own and I think he did a really excellent job."

Indeed, Baxter's atonal musical score seemed to be exactly the right fit for enhancing the mood of mystery and desolation that hangs over Castle Medina. Baxter told Randall Larson that although his scores for *House of Usher* and *Pit and the Pendulum* were each quite different, there was an overall brooding continuity between them. "*House of Usher* was a full orchestra with a choir," says Baxter, and "I used the choir to represent the ancient souls coming out of the house. In *The Pit and the Pendulum* I used some stark atonal writing, which is, to simplify somewhat, one, two or three lines in the manner of a fugue, each playing very unmelodic and unrelated notes, one to the other, which makes for very strange music. Then at the end of the film, I had the enormous, swinging pendulum sound done with the orchestra... a very slow, massive, undulating dissonance that seemed to move slowly but massively."

When the film was completed, Jim Nicholson and Sam Arkoff saw that once again Matheson and Corman had turned out a real winner and they backed it to the hilt with another all-out publicity campaign proclaiming it as "The greatest terror tale ever told." In over 11,000 play dates the film grossed nearly $4 million. The rental take that AIP collected amounted to $2.1 million, making it the most successful picture in the history of the seven-year-old company. Sam Arkoff was especially pleased with the results. "Out of all the Poe pictures," declared Arkoff, "*The Pit And The Pendulum* was the biggest grossing film of the series. It's also the one I liked the best, because it was the scariest. We had a wonderful piece of artwork for the poster (the pendulum swinging over John Kerr, drawn by artist Fred Fixler), as well as some great sets by Danny Haller."

When the film opened in August of 1961, most of the reviews were quite favorable, led most surprisingly by the highly influential *New York Times.* Howard Thompson declared: "While *The Pit and the Pendulum* is essentially another old-fashioned fright package, some credit belongs to this free adaptation for its imaginative Gothic wrapping. Atmospherically, at least—there is a striking fusion of rich colors, plushy décor and eerie music—this American International release with a small cast headed by Vincent Price is probably Hollywood's most effective Poe-style horror flavoring to date. ...Mr. Matheson's ironic plot is compact and as logical as the choice of the small cast. Against the film's elegant period appointments, ornate furniture, fire-lit tapestries, a ruby ring on a harpsichord keyboard, director-producer Roger Corman has evoked a genuinely chilling mood of horror. From the start, when abstract designs coil over the credits, the color is stunning. ...Don't expect Poe, but the taste here for poisonous cake with rich, ice-cold frosting probably would have pleased him."

Several of the more negative critical brickbats seemed to take aim at Vincent Price's performance, especially from critics who were expecting a more realistic dramatic portrayal. Howard Thompson, for instance, said, "Unfortunately, Mr. Price's florid 'acting' tilts the whole thing off realistic

Floyd Crosby, A.S.C measures the lighting for Barbara Steele

balance." And Charles Stinson's review in *The Los Angeles Times* was more akin to character assassination than instructive criticism: "Price mugs, rolls his eyes continuously and deliver his lines in such an unctuous tone that he comes near to burlesquing the role. His mad scenes were just ludicrous."

Reacting to suggestions he had gone "over the top," Price said, "If you read the script, you'll see that it required a larger-than-life performance. I felt that was really the only way to approach it. You are playing something that is unreal and you have to bring it to life. You can't just play it straight, because it won't come to life that way. So it has to be overplayed—operatic almost."

Corman acknowledged that Price had a tendency to play things on a grand scale, but says, "We tried to make it a full emotional performance, knowing that for a motion picture, an actor has to hold back a little bit, especially a stage-trained actor, as Vincent was. That was especially true for the close-ups. But I think Vincent was brilliant in that role and he was really able to convey the intensity and the madness of the character, without going over the top."

AIP was now definitely on a roll with two of their most successful films to date. Between *House of Usher* and *Pit and the Pendulum* AIP had made profits of nearly $4 million in the U.S. market alone. When the overseas take was eventually added in, it was obvious that American-International had been bitten by a real-life Gold-Bug. The result would be an ongoing series of Edgar Allan Poe pictures that would see Roger Corman direct six more adaptations from Poe's works, while AIP would continue making pictures with Poe titles for the next ten years. Reflecting back, Corman exclaimed, "Jim and Sam were really instrumental in turning American-International into the dominant independent production and distribution company in America. And *House Of Usher* was really the picture that established them. It was the first AIP movie that played alone as a single feature, whereas before that all their pictures had been sent out as double-bills."

Matheson would go on to contribute only two more screenplays to the Poe series, *Tales of Terror* and *The Raven* (which *Gauntlet Press* will publish in the spring of 2008), but stayed on as AIP's star screenwriter until Nicholson left the company in the early seventies. And in an off-screen twist, Matheson's planned novel, *House of the Dead* that served as the basis for his *Pit and the Pendulum* screenplay, ended up becoming a novel after all, when AIP turned his script into a poorly written tie-in paperback, padded with extraneous details invented by author Lee Sheridan. Now, nearly fifty years later, aficionados of Richard Matheson's screenwriting can finally read his original script for "the most diabolical classic of all time."

Lawrence French, 2012

Director Roger Corman directs Larry Turner as the young Nicholas Medina who hides underneath the staircase of the torture chamber and sees events that will haunt him forever.

THE PIT AND THE PENDULUM
(American International Pictures)

Produced & Directed by Roger Corman. Executive Producers: James H. Nicholson & Samuel Z. Arkoff. Screenplay by Richard Matheson, based on Edgar Allan Poe's "The Pit and the Pendulum." Music by Les Baxter. Director of Photography: Floyd Crosby, A.S.C. (in Panavision & Pathé-color). Production Design by Daniel Haller. Film Editor: Anthony Carras. Sound Editor: Kay Rose. Sound Recording: Roy Meadows. Costumes by Marjorie Corso. Production Manager: Bartlett A. Carre. Make-up: Ted Coodley. Special Effects: Pat Dinga. Photographic effects: Ray Mercer, Larry Butler & Don Glouner. Scenic Effects: Tom Matsumoto. Matte Paintings by Albert Whitlock. Properties: Dick Rubin. Key Grip: Chuck Hannawalt. Script supervisor: Betty Crosby. Set Dresser: Harry Reif. Gaffer: Buddy Ketzel. 1st Assistant Director: Jack Bohrer. 2nd Assistant Director: Lou Place. Unit Manager: Robert Agnew. Production Assistant: Jack Cash. Still Photographer: Frank Tanner. Construction Co-ordinator: Ross Hahn. Music Co-ordinator: Al Simms. An Alta Vista production. Filmed at California Studios (in three weeks), beginning January 4, 1961. Released in New York: August 23, 1961. Released in Los Angeles: September 28, 1961. 85 minutes.

CAST

Nicholas Medina/Sebastian Medina............. VINCENT PRICE
Francis Barnard............................. JOHN KERR
Elizabeth Barnard Medina............... BARBARA STEELE
Catherine Medina........................... LUANA ANDERS
Dr. Charles Leon ....ANTONY CARBONE
Maximillian................................... PATRICKWESTWOOD
Maria... LYNNE BERNAY
Isabella Medina............................. MARY MENZIES
Bartolomé Medina........................... CHARLES VICTOR
Nicholas (as a child)....................... LARRY TURNER

Lee Sheridan

Coming Attractions

www.ingramcontent.com/pod-product-compliance
Lightning Source LLC
Chambersburg PA
CBHW050348030726
47503CB00008B/2674

* 9 7 8 1 5 9 3 9 3 3 8 6 9 *